# No Control
## A Dark Romance
### Annie Wild

ISBN: 979-8-9884781-2-6

Cover design by: Designs by Charlyy

Printed in the United States of America

# Content Warning

This book contains dark themes and subject matter. You will find the following in this work: stalking, graphic violence, domestic violence (not between main characters), suicide idealization, graphic sex, knife play, breath play, emotional/verbal abuse (not between main characters), alcoholism, murder, gun violence, knife violence, and profanity.

Please read with discretion. Content is intended for audiences eighteen years and older.

# Dedication

To the readers who believe fictional psychopaths and red flags are romantic.

# One

## Lydia

*Good luck with the meeting today. Hopefully you'll get the contract.*

I purse my lips as I read the text from my fiancé, Mason, and then slide my phone into my bag. Usually, all my writing contracts are negotiated over email or messaging boards. It's a rarity when a potential client wants to meet in person rather than over Zoom, and it's got me on edge.

But I never turn down the chance to get out of my drabby office.

Taking a deep breath, I double check my lightly done makeup, pushing my hazel blonde hair from my face. I guess the downside to meeting in person is the lack of filters.

*Yikes.*

I slide out of my SUV and make my way into the hipster coffee shop. It was a solid forty-minute drive from my house to get here, but I didn't argue when that's where my potential client said they wanted to meet. I mentally center myself as I grab the aluminum handle, and as soon as the door swings open, I'm met with a blast of warm air and a strong scent of lattes.

I'm pretty sure this might be close to what heaven smells like.

My eyes scan the crowded place, searching for someone I've never met. My gaze stops on every single person sitting alone.

*Henry Bayne... What do you look like?*

And then my phone buzzes.

I reach into my bag and pull it out, seeing a message from Henry, himself.

> Back left. Corner booth.

My eyes flicker up, my head whips to my left.

And my heart stutters.

*That* is not what I thought Henry Bayne was going to look like—not that I thought much about his looks, anyway. But still, for some reason, my head had conjured up a middle-aged man obsessed with true crime documentaries. This man looks like the freaking serial killer in the documentary—but the Ted Bundy kind of killer. The kind you leave with...*willingly*.

"Lydia," a deep, smooth voice greets me as I numbingly make it to the booth. He stands to his feet, towering over my five-foot-three-inch frame at what must be at least six-foot- two or -three. I take in the black leather jacket, his white T- shirt, and faded jeans. His dark, nearly black hair has a natural wave to it and his gray eyes leave me feeling uneasy.

So naturally, like anyone who fails to get out much, I stare at him like an idiot.

"I got you the blonde latte." He gestures to the drink steaming opposite of his seat. "That's what you said you wanted."

*Right. In the text I sent earlier.*

But those texts don't even feel like they're from the same person anymore.

"Thanks," I choke out, ripping my eyes away from his tantaliz-ing face. I focus on pulling out my chair and taking a seat in the half-booth table setup, but my hands are shaking.

*This man flew all the way from New York City to meet with me...Why?*

I had asked myself the question over and over again, but now, I'm really wondering what the heck this guy is doing in a place like Oklahoma City—all for a meager book contract.

"So," I clear my throat like I've smoked for all thirty-three years of my life. "Let's talk about your project."

He eyes me as I reach for my latte, my fingers trembling still as they wrap around the ceramic glass. "Okay, let's talk about it." Henry leans back in the chair, folding his arms across his chest. "You know, though, you're not exactly what I pictured."

*Right back at ya, bud.*

But instead of speaking my mind, I take a long sip of my drink, letting it burn the shit out of my tongue. "What were you expecting, Mr. Bayne?"

He chuckles, though his tone has an edge that serves to further unnerve me. "Don't call me Mr. Bayne. Henry is preferred."

"I apologize, Henry," I say quickly, ignoring the rush of heat in my cheeks. I use the moment to dig into my bag and retrieve my notebook. I flip it open and click my pen, feeling a little more confident with it in my hand.

*I can always stab him if he tries anything.*

"I was thinking that we follow my initial thoughts."

"A dark thriller?"

"Yeah, similar to your own works."

I freeze, looking up from my scribbled notes—no one knows that I write for myself on the side, and most of my audience is, well, women. "I'm not sure I know what you're talking about..."

He smiles, flashing me a set of perfect pearly whites. "I know you write under a pen name. The depravity in your work appeals to me, and you're quite successful with your own literature—why are you still ghostwriting?"

I shift in my seat, feeling the urge to squirm under his heated gaze. "Um...I guess I haven't reached the point where they pay the bills yet. I also like helping other people achieve their writing goals, I guess."

Henry nods, albeit a slow bob of his head. "I see. Well, hopefully, this project will change that."

"How so?" I don't bother to hide my confusion. "We've already spoken about the agreed rate of five cents per word. That's—"

His tongue runs along his bottom lip, and my eyes follow it like bait, watching his perfectly shaped mouth say, "I'll pay you significantly more if you'll abide by my terms."

I blink a couple of times, recognizing the change in his tone. It's as intriguing as it is intimidating. "And what are your terms?"

"I believe in order to write the best book, we should have a close working relationship. The setting is around Los Angeles, and I'd prefer you move there temporarily while the book is written. I have a place there. You can return home when the first draft is complete."

I narrow my eyes. "I thought you lived in New York City..."

He nods. "I do. I live both places, but I'd like for this novel to be set there. It's winter, too, and trust me, you'll appreciate the warmer temperatures of LA."

"I..." my voice trails off as I consider the offer. "I assume I'll need a temporary apartment?"

"Not necessary. My home is big enough to accommodate you."

I open my mouth to say something, but nothing comes out for a few beats as his eyes hold mine. "I need to speak with my fiancé about this, before I agree to anything."

Something shifts in his eyes, and it leaves me feeling cold inside. "Very well." He reaches into a bag I never realized was sitting next to him, pulling out a thick packet of papers. "Here's the contract. Feel free to spend the evening mulling it over. My flight leaves tomorrow evening at eight. You have until then to make your decision."

I nod as he pushes the contract across the table to me, the edges bumping into my fingertips. "What about the rate?"

He chuckles a dark, borderline insidious laugh. "It's all in there. Let me know what you think, Lydia. We'll speak soon." He slides out of the booth gracefully, slinging the black backpack over his shoulder. "I hope you truly consider my offer. I'd hate to see you turn down something of this caliber."

I gaze up at him as he towers over the booth, his frame naturally muscular but not bulky. His arrogance challenges his charisma—in a bad way. "Of course. Thank you for considering my services."

Henry's lips curl into a wicked smile. "Of course. It was a pleasure to finally meet you. Have a nice evening, Lydia."

My eyes follow him as he leaves the coffee shop, and I realize that I might be the only one gawking at him now. Everyone else seems to be unaware of his presence—not so different than I was when I entered the place. It was as if he had been invisible...

That was, until I locked gazes with him.

Now, however, I feel as though I've been shaken until my brain detached from my skull. But as he disappears into the late afternoon sun, I snap back to reality and grab the contract. Part of me wants to rip it up and throw it in the trash, but I have a deep-seated fear that the man might somehow know. So, I shove it into my messenger bag and shake it off.

Henry Bayne has left me riddled with questions, but there's one thing I'm one hundred percent sure of...

*There is no way in* hell *I'm writing a book for him.*

# Two

## Henry

*She's fucking engaged.*

I sit in my rented black Tahoe, staring at the steering wheel, anger burning in my chest. With all the research, time spent, and all the long sleepless nights of studying Lydia, I *never* knew the woman was betrothed to someone else.

And this is a big problem. Huge problem.

Because while I'm the kind of man who gets what I want, there are some lines that I'll never cross—and being a homewrecker is one of them. But, the painful thought of Lydia's body being touched by another man, threatens to initiate the darkest side of me. And to add to such murderous temptations, she's *engaged* to him. There's a fucking rock on her hand.

*How was this missed?*

Pulling out my phone, I scroll to Jude's name, clicking it without a second of hesitation. I listen to it ring in my ear, my eyes focused on the exit of the coffee shop. Lydia still hasn't left, and as I check my watch, I see that it's been eleven minutes since I abandoned her at the booth.

"Hey," Jude's voice grates my nerves. "How'd it go? Mission accomplished?"

"She's *engaged.*"

"Yeah?"

"What do you mean, *yeah*?" I growl, gripping the steering wheel so hard my knuckles turned white. "I gave you one job, Jude. *One. Fucking. Job.*"

"And I did it? Just like always?"

"I asked for everything on her."

"Yeah..."

"So why did you fail to add that?"

"I didn't."

"It's not in the file," I sneer, losing my patience.

"It's not? Aw shit, hang on then. It should've been in the digital file..." His voice trails off, replaced by the incessant clicking of his fingers on a keyboard. It would be annoying, but lucky for me, I'm given the best distraction yet as Lydia steps out of the coffee shop...

And appears more paranoid than an amateur drug mule.

Her blonde hair hits just below her shoulders, though the winds whip it violently around her face. I bite my lip as I imagine that hair fisted in my hand, the strands cutting off the circulation of my fingers. Lydia glances around the area before damn near running to her SUV, parked right out front.

*Shit.*

I knew I'd gotten under her skin, but I hadn't been out to terrify her—not yet, anyway.

"Damnit, Henry, I'm sorry," Jude groans. "I put it in the wrong file."

"Big mistake for the best hacker I know." I grit my teeth, wishing like hell Lydia's windows weren't tinted so darkly. She's clearly the kind of woman who doesn't like eyes on her...

But she's never getting rid of mine.

"I'm sending it over now. What's the payout on her? Hopefully I didn't screw that up for you. I didn't even get the link—I didn't think we took on women, anyway."

I blink for a moment, not registering his question as Lydia backs out of the parking spot. "I'm going to put you on speaker." I shift the call to the Bluetooth system of the rental, and then pull away from the curb, following Lydia at a good distance. I let a few cars get in between us.

It's better not to add to her newly developed paranoia.

"Henry?" Jude's voice plays over the loudspeaker.

"Yeah?"

"What's the payout on her?" Jude repeats his question. "She's not the normal target...And I didn't think you took on women?"

"I don't," I say flatly, turning onto the entrance ramp of the interstate.

"Okay..."

"She's not a target."

*Well, not that kind, anyway.*

"So then what are you doing with this poor writer?"

*Making her mine.*

"I don't know yet," I lie, taking the exit behind her. I have no idea where she's going, but it's not home. I click my tongue, not having intended to follow her like this. I've waited months to meet her in person, carefully planning how this was going to go, and now, it's been ruined by the presence of a fiancé that I stupidly didn't know existed.

*It's a major fuck up.*

And the consequence of stalking from a distance. And putting my trust in Jude.

"This is the one your sister likes?" Jude's tone is that of caution. "She gave you the books, right? I saw them on your shelf. Lydia writes those creepy thrillers with the twisted romance. Kind of like a starry-eyed Romeo and Juliet, only they survive."

"Yeah, that's her."

"Just like all the other dark romances out there. It's amazing what these women are into."

I don't say anything to that. Yeah, I mean, Lydia is one of many when it comes to writing books. But unlike the others—at least to me—there *is* something different about her. Maybe it's the mystery that surrounds her true identity, hidden away from the world. She never puts herself out there, even though she most definitely could. And I have to admit, Lydia is the first woman that's ever caught my attention.

With those stunning, yet troubled, jade eyes.

"You should be careful." Jude's warning comes as a surprise. "I don't know what you're doing with this woman, but she's not from our world, Henry. She might write dark, but even in the writing, you can tell she's not like us. She's just—"

"That's enough," I snap, cutting him off as I watch Lydia turn into an Italian restaurant. I drive past the lot, and then whip into an office supply store a quarter mile further south. I want to be as close as possible, but if she's truly beside herself with worry, she's going to be watching for familiar vehicles.

And I can't risk that.

I need her to go over that contract. *And agree to it.*

Because even if I can't have her body...

I'll be damned if I don't take her fucking soul.

Putting the vehicle in park, I'm two lots over now, the SUV hidden by a row of bushes. They hinder my view, but not so much that I can't make out what's going on—and in the pit of my stomach, I already have a good idea of what's about to happen.

And sure enough, a white pickup truck pulls in beside her. My jaw tenses as I watch a tall, slender man slide out of the driver's side of the truck. He's got blond hair and a clean- shaven face, exposing his jutted chin. He's an office dweller based on his slacks and button down. With a scrutinizing gaze, I find myself critiquing him in ways that I don't usually, but with that comes my imagination, comforting me with violent images of tearing the man to shreds.

That would be *one* way to have Lydia to myself.

But that would leave her mourning a lost love. And while I, myself, can't seem to figure out how to fall in love, if this is going to work between us, Lydia, at least, will not love another man.

A cramp skyrockets up my wrist as I watch the dreaded scene play out in front of me. The man greets Lydia, and she looks up at him like a puppy, her eyes shimmering beneath the setting sun. My jaw aches from how tightly wound it is, and I brace for what I believe is coming... But it doesn't happen.

He doesn't even bother to lean in and kiss those full lips of hers. He simply side-hugs her like a friend and then drops his arm, leading the way into the restaurant. Lydia is left to follow him, her shoulders slumped, and her expression giving away her moment of disappointment.

*Interesting.*

I pull my phone back out from where I sat it on the console, scrolling to the updated file.

"You know I'm still here, right?" Jude's voice comes over the speaker.

"Yeah," I mutter, tapping the folder to view the new contents. "And you'll stay here until I'm done with this."

He sighs but doesn't protest. After all, he screwed this up in the first place. I should've never relied on him to gather it all, but I had a high-profile target to take care of that took months of stalking and waiting. The moment the job was complete, I'd taken over Lydia... And trusted that Jude had done his job.

*Stupid me.*

But all thoughts about it dissipate as I begin to flip through the information Jude failed to put in the right place. I chew the inside of my cheek until I taste copper, scrolling through sickening pictures of the two of them together.

*Mason Prewitt.*

I read up on his stats, unimpressed to find that he's a car salesman at a local dealership—though that's just his most recent acquisition. As it turns out, Mr. Prewitt is a job hopper...

With plenty of downtime between.

"Talk about some low expectations," I mumble, mostly to myself. She can do so much better.

"Yeah, the guy is a real piece of work. They live together at a house Lydia owns—but he does rent an apartment about twenty minutes away. I think she pays most of the bills when her beau doesn't have a job. However, in her defense, when they first got together, the guy appeared top notch. He was first of his graduating class at the state university, and he seemed to be going places with high profile internships and all that academic jazz."

"Hmm," I say, as if I actually give a shit at all about *Mason Prewitt.*

"They've been engaged for about three months, and from what I've gathered, I can't find an actual date set for a wedding. I'm not sure which one is holding off on that."

*Hopefully, Lydia.*

"He's close with her family, but you know, she doesn't appear to be."

"You just trying to piss me off?"

"No...It's just the same information I always give to you. Henry, as a friend, is this..." Jude's voice trails off in a way that catches my attention. "Is this a romantic interest?"

"With Mason?" I break out into a sardonic laugh. "Absolutely not."

# Three

## Lydia

"So, this is the contract," I say, pulling it from my bag and handing it over to Mason, who's munching on a breadstick already. "I just...I don't know. The guy kind of made me feel...uncomfortable."

"Any time you have to talk to someone in person, you feel that way," Mason thrums, taking the papers from my hand. "But I'll look at it. It's not like you *have* to take this job, anyway. You have plenty of other options. You just never take them."

"Yeah," I mutter, running my fingers along the sticky tabletop. I don't know who was in charge of cleaning it, but they didn't do a spectacular job. However, it serves as a short-lived distraction from the sting of his words. "I also could take the free time in my schedule to work on my own stuff."

"What stuff?"

"You know, the series I started working on," I try to prod his memory. "I told you all about them."

"Yeah, right. Sorry. You know I don't like to read that stuff."

"Right. History only." I keep my voice calm and collected, my eyes shifting out the window we're seated beside. It's nearly dark out now, and I find myself replaying the meeting with Henry over and over again in my head.

*There's just something about him...*

"This is wild!" Mason exclaims, dropping his breadstick to the ceramic plate. "Did you see this, Lyd? A fucking hundred grand for a book!"

"What?" I reach for the papers, snatching it from his hands. "That can't be right. That's like celebrity memoir writing..." But as my eyes land on the bolded amount, a lump forms in my throat. It *is* right.

*And half gets paid upfront.*

"What kind of services does this guy want from you?" Mason's dark eyes meet mine, and I catch myself hesitating. "Well?"

I force a shrug. "Just a book."

"What kind of book? You've never been paid anything close to this."

"I don't know...Kind of like the ones I write for myself, but without the romance?" That last part is an assumption. Henry Bayne didn't strike me as the kind of guy who wanted romance—and we'd only discussed thrillers in our previous mundane chats.

*But all my books are centered around romance...*

I bite down on my bottom lip, feeling the heat build in my cheeks as I think about Henry reading those stories. "I really don't know."

"I bet he wants to sleep with you."

I can't stop the laugh that slips from my throat. *If anything, he probably wants to murder me.* That was a vibe I got from him.

But then again, I can be a little mistrusting with all the crime docs and morbid books I read. Maybe I should back off on those.

"So, this guy just reads your work," Mason muses. "And now he thinks you're worth a hundred grand? For this kind of money, why wouldn't the guy just take some writing courses and do it himself. That's what I'd do. It's not that hard to write a book—not like yours, anyway. Aren't they like a fourth-grade reading level?"

I sigh, pushing my hair behind my ear. "I don't know." *But you're being an asshole about this.*

As much as I want to, there's never a point in arguing with Mason. He thinks what he's going to think, and I've learned not to argue with him. It only leads to more problems. And I have enough on my mind right now.

"Is he going to pay for you to move?"

"It's probably in the contract..."

Mason huffs. "I'm going to read through it. Make sure you don't miss anything. This isn't really your strong suit. I know you tend to skim over things." He continues to scan through the pages, and I sit quietly, my eyes on the food that sits in front of me.

I pick at the fettucine alfredo, taking a bite every so often, waiting for Mason to make it through the contract. I try not to focus on anything he's said. Mason's gotten meaner as the years have passed, and it's definitely rooted in his own failures. And sometimes—as in every day—I question why I'm still with him. But for some reason, it's worse than ever today.

"This guy really covers his bases."

*I'm not surprised.*

I may have only spent fifteen minutes with Henry in a coffee shop and exchanged a max of five messages, but I still somehow know he's thorough. He had to have been to figure out my pen name...

Though I'm sure that's not as hard as it seems.

"The contract really appears to be in your favor. You better sign it and get to packing. You're stupid not to take this."

I stop, my fork hanging midair as my irritation grows. "I already told you I don't want to do it."

"Why not?"

"He's kind of...off." I don't mention the fact that he gave me serial killer vibes. That'll just lead to Mason telling me that I spend too much time watching documentaries about them—and he might actually be right with that jab.

"Yeah? He might be a little off, as you put it, but all his information is right here in this contract. Some guy who's out to exploit you isn't going to do that."

"It could be fake."

"It's not fake."

"How do you know?" I demand, setting my fork down with an obnoxious clatter. "You can't tell by just reading the contract that all the information there is legitimate."

"No, but Google can."

I nearly roll my eyes at the snarky reply, watching Mason as he pulls out his phone. "You can't trust the internet."

"There're background checks you can run on here."

*Yeah, and plenty of sickos have clean slates.*

"I'll pay the five dollars," he chuckles, typing away on his phone. "This kind of money could really change things for us. Think of the wedding we could have."

My stomach sours at the comment. *Now he brings it up.* He's been putting the wedding off since he proposed. He wouldn't even agree to a date two years from now. Not to mention, no matter how many times I try to tell myself marrying Mason is the right thing to do, something in my gut just...doesn't agree. I only said yes because of the pressure from family—and feeling like my biological clock is ticking.

Though, I'm starting to wonder if either of those are worth it. I might rather my ovaries shrivel up and die than procreate with him.

*Why am I still putting up with him, again? And why does it feel like I just realized this?*

"It's loading," Mason slides his phone across the table so that I can see the screen. "You'll see anything there is to know about him."

"I don't think these things work like that..." my voice trails off as the page displays results—a surprising amount. I pick up his phone, my heart suddenly pounding in my ears. It's got all of Henry's information, including his New York address and another in Los Angeles. "Is this the same one on the contract?" I hold out Mason's phone so he can check.

"Yeah, it is. The phone number is the same, too." Mason grins, giving me that *I told you so* face.

"I still don't know..."

"Ask for more money then."

"What if he wants more than just a book from me?" I blurt out suddenly and my face grows hot as a result. I blame Mason for putting it in my head in the first place.

He raises an eyebrow. "What do you think, then? He's just hiring you because you're hot? I'm pretty sure he can get a lot of women for much less than a hundred g's."

My heart sinks, regardless of my resentment. "You're right."

"I don't mean that the way you're taking it," Mason says quickly, reaching across the table and grabbing my hand. "I just mean, if he's out for sex, he can get that from just about anyone, probably. It's not like there's not a million fish in the sea."

I nod. "Yeah...But hypothetically," I begin, unable to hide my curiosity, "what if he did? What would we do?" I don't know why I'm asking the question. It's not like I'd ever cross such a line. But my mind keeps toying with the idea, anyway.

"You'd do it," Mason pulls his hand away, bursting into a fit of laughter. "I don't know why you wouldn't. Like I said, slap on an extra fifty-thousand, and I'd be fine with it. I think we'd handle it just fine. Money is money."

I blink a couple of times, a thrum of disbelief rolling through my body. "You know that'd mean he'd sleep with me, right?"

Mason makes a face. "Obviously, but come on. It's a fling. It's not like you love him or something. It'd just be for the cash. You could take a dick for that. We could pay off all my student loans."

My brows shoot up as a surprising amount of anger explodes in my chest. "Pay off your student loans? Seriously? That's messed up, Mason." *He's seriously going to pimp me out for his student loan repayment?*

The ick is strong even for Mason, who pushes my boundaries all the time. But maybe this is one push too far. Way too far.

"What?" Mason shrugs. "I don't see what's so bad about that. Those student loans are what's setting us back so far. Well, that and your car payment."

*You have to be kidding me.*

My hands turn to fists. "My car payment is only three hundred dollars a month..."

"That's still a significant amount and let's not forget about the other shit you buy whenever you feel like it. I spend money, too," he adds quickly, putting his hands up in surrender. "But you get what I'm saying. It costs money to live a nice life. You'll be taking this job. Besides, the way you talk about your books, you're into those creepy kinds of guys."

My top teeth bear down into the flesh of my bottom lip, and I push my plate back from me. "I'm not doing it, and if I did agree to it, it wouldn't be your money to do anything with. I'm tired of you relying on my check to pay for everything. You won't even set a wedding date." I slide toward the edge of the booth, done with everything about this freaking night. And the last six years.

"Where the fuck are you going?" he growls, grabbing for my wrist.

I jerk it away before his hand connects. "Home." I snatch the contract from the table as I stand to my feet. "And you can stay at your place tonight. I need time to think about this."

"About what?" Mason sneers. "You're really going to break up our six-year relationship over some stupid comment?"

"Yes," I snap at him, on the verge of losing my shit right there in the restaurant. "You're fine with pimping me out to some guy you've never even met for the money to pay off your student loans. It's the last straw. I'm done with it."

"Well, when you put it that way, it does sound bad," he chuckles, shrugging. "Just sit down. We'll talk about it. I can call the guy if you're really that scared."

*Forget this.*

I spin on my heels, ignoring Mason calling after me. I've spent the last half-decade of my life waiting for him to straighten up. Granted, the first few years, he showered me with affection, putting me on a pedestal and making me feel like a queen. But even then, the red flags were there in the form of gaslighting, narcissism, and physical intimidation on the rare occasion we fought. His apologies just somehow made it right in my young, naïve head, and by the time I realized it, I felt trapped. Everyone told me he would figure it out, too—that he just needed to find his place in the world.

*Bullshit.*

I'm tired of always being hurt, and maybe this hiccup is an excuse to finally pull the plug. He's always been a dick to me, even if he was sly about it.

*"He's a jerk, but he loves you."*

*"He might be a little narcissistic, but he's working on it."*

The words of my family, friends, and his family reverberate in my head, but I'm done. I have my out, and I'm taking it.

*Screw 'em all. Let my family hate me.*

My hands connect with the door handle creating a loud pop, and I push it open, welcoming the cold air. I head straight for my car, shoving the contract back into my bag. I'm not bending for anyone anymore—not Mason, not Henry.

"Lydia, wait!" Mason shouts as I reach the driver's side door. "I'm sorry for saying that shit about sleeping with the guy or whatever. It was just a joke. Come on."

I pause, turning to face Mason as he jogs toward me. "It wasn't a joke. I want space, Mason. Leave me alone."

"You're kidding," he pants as he stops a few feet from me. "You're overreacting."

"No, I'm not," I say flatly.

"Come on, Lydia. You're being so stupid right now. Every time you do this, you regret it. You know sometimes I can be crude. I don't mean it—I never do."

I glare at him, shaking my head. "Go sleep at your own place." I climb into the driver's seat and grab the inside door handle. "It's over."

And before he can say anything at all, I slam the door.

*Right in his freaking face.*

# Four

## Henry

I tilt my head as the scene plays out in the parking lot. I swear, I should've popped some popcorn for this. It looks like there's some turmoil in their picture-perfect romance, and I wait patiently as her SUV peels out of the parking lot.

"What'd you do, Mason?" I chuckle, putting my car in reverse. The guy throws his hands up in the air, and I recognize the exasperation in his body language. My guess is my contract got a rise out of him.

But why? I don't know.

And I don't have time to chat with Mason about it—nor do I want to. I need to tail Lydia, and from the way some of the restaurant staff has joined Mason in the parking lot, it looks like he still has a bill to pay. I drive right by the chaos, half-tempted to wave at the asshat.

But I don't.

Lydia is *moving*.

I punch in the coordinates of her house, already knowing where she's headed as she takes the exit onto the turnpike. Again, I don't want to cause any unnecessary fear in her right now. I'll have to be extra careful in this pursuit, and for that reason, I keep a solid distance between us. If I scare her too much, I might have to resort to much less amicable terms than those in the contract.

And I'd hate to do that.

But I will if I have to.

Lydia Waters is the answer to the question I've been asking myself since I survived the night my parents were murdered. After reading her books, I wanted to solve the mystery of who she was, feeling like she wrote the *same* man in every single book. He might take a different dark twist, kink, or scenario, but regardless, I see myself on the page—and I want to know *why*.

I mean, is the woman manifesting me? Could someone actually want *me*?

But then the more I dig into her, I get lost in the complexities of the way she hides herself from the world, covering her tracks like someone is out to get her. And when I finally saw that face in person tonight, I just...

I fucking *knew* I was right. And now, I want to know what happens if I get a taste of her. She seems so warm, like a cabin with a blazing fireplace in the middle of a blizzard. Can she cut through the cold in me?

I think she might, and I've never even cared until *her*.

"Why are you going to her house?" Jude's voice comes over the speaker, jarring me from my thoughts. "This is a bad idea."

"I never have bad ideas." Though right now, I hate the fact he always has my GPS coordinates.

"Your arrogance is almost charming. But really, what are you going to do? I don't want our partnership put in jeopardy because you can't keep your dick in your pants."

I make a face. "Don't be so vulgar. It's unbecoming."

"Says the man who enjoys knife play for a living."

"Not an actual kink of mine," I chuckle. *That I know of.* I've never bothered with women enough to even know.

But I intend to figure that out with Lydia.

"This isn't like you, and it's got me a little nervous."

"I'm hanging up if you keep this up," I grunt, taking the rural exit. I let myself fall about a mile or so behind Lydia. I need time to scope the place out, and from what I know, her property is very secluded.

And that makes it *way* too easy for me.

"You're going to terrify her."

"Nah, not tonight," I say, easing off the gas as I turn onto a dark gravel road. She made a forty-five-minute drive into thirty-five. She's definitely angry. "I just want to keep an eye on her. She's got until tomorrow night at eight to accept the offer."

There's silence on the other end of the phone for a few beats. "*What* offer, Henry?"

"To write a book. That's what she does for a living. You know that."

"Oh shit," he groans. "You're a sick fuck, baiting her in like this."

"It's the easiest, most consensual choice," I mutter as her house comes into view. Her car is already parked outside, the engine off and the lights on in the front room. The house is a nice little one-story log cabin. It could use some maintenance, but I have a feeling Mason is worthless in that area.

And lucky for me, it's surrounded by thick woods.

"You know, you could've asked her on a date." Jude's voice is like nails on a chalkboard as I turn down the dead-end road about five hundred feet from her property line.

"Who lives in this house?" I ask, ignoring his advice and focusing on the task at hand. I'm not well-suited for *dating*. It requires too much emotional patience. And that is in low supply for me.

"Are you talking about the trailer just to the southeast?"

"Yeah, that one."

"That's the only neighbor she has, and..." his voice trails off. "The old woman died about two months ago. Family hasn't made a decision to sell yet."

*Perfect.*

I pull into the grass covered driveway, long having killed the head-lights. Navigating around to the back of the trailer, I stop and put it in park. "This is probably just as nice as my hotel room. I'll talk to you later."

"Wait—"

I hang up before he can say whatever it is he thinks I need to hear. I have a good feeling it's another one of his well-meant warn-ings—that I won't heed. Nothing bad is happening to Lydia tonight. I reach for my black hoodie, removing my leather jacket and sliding it on. I'd hate to be seen in familiar clothing. Picking up my phone, I scroll to the text thread with Lydia. There're only three messages.

> It's Henry. What would you like to drink? I'll order. I'm here early.

> Oh! I'll have a blonde latte. Thank you!

> Back left. Corner booth.

I run my tongue along my bottom lip, half tempted to ask if she's had a chance to go over the contract. I need her to agree to it—to make the first step easy. We had only exchanged a few messages outside of those texts, and they'd all been discussions about writing a thriller book for a new publishing company I had no intention of starting. It's minimal contact, and I intend for that to change. *Soon.*

But it's a game of patience. No emotions required.

And for that reason, I exit out of the thread and shove my phone into my pocket. Typically, I'd use a burner for something this dicey, but I'm not letting Lydia slip away. Besides, *Henry Bayne* is a clean man, making his money through tech investments.

Silently, I slip out of the car, the cold air hardly putting me off. I reach for the neck gaiter hidden beneath the neckline of my hoodie. I pull it up over my nose, flip my hood up, and glide through the knee-high grass. I prefer my mask. But it's back at the hotel room.

The wind is whipping tonight, and it works in my favor as I edge through the woods, crossing the barbed wire fence onto Lydia's property. She's got a stunning eighty acres surrounding her house that she inherited from family, and it's mostly wooded. I stop as soon as the house comes into view. Right now, I'm positioned to the side of it, and so I make my way around to the back, hoping to get a better line of sight. None of the windows provide me with an internal view.

She keeps her blinds closed, apparently.

*Good for her.*

I mean, you never know who might be creeping around in the night. I chuckle silently to myself, rounding the back of the house while staying a good fifteen feet back in the cover of the thick woods.

And that's when I catch sight of her.

Standing on the back porch, her arms are wrapped tightly around her body. "Go potty, Duke!" she calls out into the night.

I furrow my brow right as my phone vibrates in my pocket.

I pull it out, seeing a text from Jude.

She's got a dog. Be careful.

*Well, that would've been nice to know.*

I shove it back in my pocket, trying to get eyes on just what kind of canine I'm up against—but she's all I can focus on. Her hair is now piled on top of her head in a messy bun, and the shorts she's got on show off her muscular thighs and round ass. She's a runner, but it's easy to see she carries thick muscles on her lower half.

And I'm here for it.

*Damnit. Don't get distracted.*

As much as I'd love to fantasize mentally bending her over those porch rails, tonight is not the night for that. She has less than twenty-four hours to let me know if she's accepting my offer, and the tension between her and her *fiancé* has me hoping she's going to come willingly.

And leave him in the dust for me to annihilate.

If it were up to me, I'd hunt down every single man who ever fucking *looked* at her, plucking their eyes right out of their skull with the tip of my knife.

But I have to be realistic.

I should probably only focus on the men who've actually touched her.

A light growl in the dark nips at my thoughts.

*Ah, there it is.*

I narrow my eyes, squinting at the shaggy mutt of a dog a few feet out in front of me. He's some sort of hound mixed with a retriever, maybe? He's got a deep golden coat. No matter how pretty the dog is, he's not nearly as happy to see me as I hoped he'd be.

"Hey, buddy," I say softly, keeping my voice at a whisper. I glance back at Lydia, who's eyes are on her phone, back angled toward us.

*Perfect.*

Duke, I assume, takes a step toward me, his dark muzzle still curled in a snarl. As much as I hate to see he's not welcoming me with open arms, it's a win he's not barking at me. I need to keep this up.

I dig into my pocket, grabbing my protein bar. "This probably isn't good for you, but it's the fastest way to make a truce—I'm gonna be here awhile." I snap off the end of it, and toss it toward him, letting it hit the leaves just in front of him. His body jerks, but even in the dim moonlight, I see his nose twitching.

Duke sniffs the ground and inhales the damn bar like he hasn't eaten in week—and then he sits, tilting his head as a means of asking for more.

"That was too easy," I chuckle in a whisper as I grab another piece, this time offering it to him from my hand. He takes it, and once he's done wolfing it down, I'm able to pet the top of his head. The dog relaxes, sniffing all over the bottom half of my jeans while I pat down his back, feeling the silky long hair. He's definitely a strange mix, but I'm not one to judge a book by its cover.

And he's nice enough.

It's not something I'd normally do, but I'll let her bring him along, *I guess.*

"Duke!" a voice calls out, catching my attention—and Duke's. I glance up to see Lydia peering off the porch into the night. "Where are you? It's cold out here."

"You better go," I whisper, stepping back from the dog. He follows me, and my shoulders drop. "Go on." I try to wave him off, but he only starts wagging his tail harder.

"Duke, don't make me come looking for you," Lydia groans into the stillness of the night. "Come on." She whistles one last time, and when the dog still doesn't come, she heads off the back porch.

*Shit.*

# Five

## Lydia

*Where is he?*

I squint into the darkness, my eyes still adjusting from my phone screen to the blackness surrounding my backyard. "Duke!" I call my dog's name again, wrapping my arms tighter around my body. My thin cardigan isn't enough for the chilly evening, and my slippers hardly keep my feet warm. "Come on, boy, it's cold out here."

It's unlike him to take off, and I worked hard to teach him to recall. Besides, he *hates* the cold. I trudge to the edge of the woods and hesitate. Despite loving to hike through the trees in the daylight, there's something about the pitch-black forest that turns me off at night.

I freeze as I hear a twig snap to my right, and whip my head in the direction, my heart kicking up a notch in my chest. Breathing in slowly, I can't make out anything in the shadows.

*I should've brought my gun.*

It's a silly thought, though I do own enough for a small arsenal. Living in the middle of nowhere, it's nice to have my own sort of security. And besides, I do occasionally enjoy hunting—but they're no help when they're locked in a safe inside the house.

Crunching leaves echo through the night, and I have the sobering realization that I'm lingering in the open, the light from the electric pole shining directly on me. If there's anything sinister in the dark cover of the trees, I might as well be parading right to my death.

And that trips my heart into a panic.

I start to back up as the sounds grow, sending my head into a spiral of fear. I nearly trip over a pot of dead flowers when Duke emerges from the trees, excitedly wagging his tail at me.

"You scared me!" I run my fingers over my face, letting out a sharp breath. "Jeez." I shudder as I glance toward the darkness behind him. I don't know why I'm on edge—other than just the stress of the evening. My phone buzzes as I turn to head back to the house, and I glance down to see Mason's face light up the screen.

*Nope.*

I reject the call and stomp up the porch steps, rolling my eyes. He's called multiple times, and I've answered none of them—which won't change. It's over between us. Of that, I'm sure. Six years down the drain.

But good riddance.

I'm sure the heartbreak will set in eventually, but right now, I'm over it. Duke and I pad across the old wooden deck, but as I reach for the sliding glass door, I freeze. The hair on the back of my neck stands to attention as a chill runs down my spine. Alarm bells ring through my head, my breath picking up. I glance over my shoulder, bracing to see something.

Or *someone.*

But there's nothing in the eerie orange glow of the pole light.

I do my best to shove my fear to the side as I slide the door open, the warmth beckoning me in with promises of safety. "I think I'm going crazy," I mutter under my breath as I close the door behind me, flipping the lock. I grab the metal bar I cut to fit in the track, working as a secondary lock on the door, and jam it in the space.

Mason always said it was overkill, and the intrusive thought of him makes me frown. I pull out my phone, scrolling to Emma's name. Normally, I would just text her, but tonight?

The silence in my house is deafening.

"Hello?" she answers on the third ring, her voice groggy.

"Are you sleeping right now?" I ask as I pull the curtain closed over my glass door, breathing a sigh of relief. If Bigfoot is out there lurking in the woods, at least he can't see me. I never understood the women in horror movies living with their lives on full blast through open windows—we can do better.

"I was," Emma says, letting out a yawn. "Jared went for another one of those late-night runs."

"Hmm," I mutter.

"Yeah, I think he's still seeing his secretary." Emma's voice is blank and matter of fact. "It is what it is. I don't wanna talk about it."

I sigh, hearing the defeat in her voice. "Well, speaking of shitty men..."

"What did he do this time? I swear, he's a—"

"I broke up with him," I cut her off, watching Duke climb into the brown leather recliner and circling until he finally curls up in a ball. "I guess I finally couldn't take his shit anymore."

"Good for you!" Emma's voice brightens. "I'm proud of you, Lydia. I always knew he was a shitty human being. I'm glad you got out before it became even more complicated. Trust me, a marriage license makes it a lot harder."

I frown, feeling sympathetic. "You'll figure it out."

"Maybe, but let's not talk about it tonight. Why don't you tell me what happened with Mason? I could use the distraction."

Just as I open my mouth to spill the tea, Duke's head pops up from its resting place, a low growl filling the room. "Um."

"You okay?" Emma's voice sounds distant as my focus remains on my dog, still growling at the door.

"Yeah, I'm fine," I say, pushing myself up from the couch. "Duke just heard something."

"I don't know how you stand living out there in the middle of nowhere."

"It doesn't bother me." I try to shrug off the jitters creeping through my body as I near the curtain, though they still linger. Duke emits another low snarl as I reach out, my finger hovering over the outdoor lightswitch.

"You definitely sound bothered."

"Nope." I pop the word out just as I flip the back porch light on. And I *swear* I hear the wood creak.

Duke lets out a bark, and I rip the curtain back, preparing for the worst.

But there's nothing.

I pull the drapery back into place and let out a sigh. "I think I'm just paranoid right now. I had a weird day."

"Expand on that."

I plop back down on the couch and spend the next twenty minutes telling the entire story from the time I sat down for coffee with the mysterious—and kind of scary—Henry to right then, sitting there talking to her.

"So..." Emma's voice trails off for a few moments. "Are you gonna do it?"

"Uh, *no.*"

"Why not? Can you imagine what kind of book *that* would make? Going off to write some novel for some hot scary stranger? I mean, you're single now."

"I don't want to die," I say tersely. "Like I told you, I think something is off with him."

"Yeah, and I'm sure there're plenty of people who think there's something *off* with us, too. We write weird literature for a living."

"Touché," I laugh, but then pause. "In theory, it seems like it would be adventurous and fun, I just...I don't know. Being stuck in a city I've never been to with a man I *barely* know sounds like the beginnings of a horror movie."

"Thriller, probably, but yeah," Emma giggles. "I would still do it. You said all his information is in the contract. Like go have wild, crazy sex—and let me live vicariously through you."

"As appealing as that sounds...*no.* Like I said, it's too good to be true."

She sighs on the other end of the line. "Or maybe you're just not giving yourself enough credit, Lydia. You're a great writer, and you've worked with some big names. Maybe the guy knows that, and he cares about his book. He wants to work closely with you on the project? I feel like that's how it used to be before technology advanced."

"I don't know... What if..." I can barely bring myself to say it aloud again. "What if he wants *more?*"

"You mean, he wants you close so he can sleep with you? Like what Mason said?"

"Yeah," I mumble. "I know it sounds insane. He just planted the seed in my head, and now I can't let it go."

"Maybe because you want it to be like that?"

"No." *Maybe.*

"Maybe Henry was a good reason to call it off with Mason? Maybe it was the push you needed to get out."

I run my fingers through my hair and groan, feeling exasperated. "I don't know. The whole contract thing was the reason I broke up with Mason—but it was coming. We knew it was. I just...needed a reason to call it off. He never treated me all that great..."

"He treated you like shit," Emma says softly. "You deserved better. No matter what your family says about him."

"Yeah, but now I'll probably never have kids."

"Well, it's better to have them with the right person when you're older than with the wrong person when you're in your *prime*—but really, I think you should consider the book contract. Or, if you don't like the terms, just negotiate ones that you're more comfortable with."

"I guess I could mention it. I just hate confrontation."

"You can do it. The money would be worth it."

I bite down on my lip, my eyes sweeping to the kitchen in desperate need of updates. "It would be helpful..."

"And you won't have Mason chipping in anymore—not that he did all that much. The man was unreliable at best."

"I guess," I say, a slight pang of heartache tugging at me. Even though I know I'd fallen out of love with him—or something of the sorts—when he refused to set a date for the wedding, it still leaves me feeling lonely knowing it's over. It's the pain of starting all over, and no contract, no matter how big the number, can change that.

"I know it's been hard for you," Emma continues, "and it's going to be hard moving forward, but you can do this."

"He only proposed because of the pressure my family put on him."

"And that's why you're not close to your own freaking family anymore. They should've let it die, not try to shove marriage down your throat. And *he* was the problem the whole time, anyway."

"I know," I sigh. As much as she's right, however, I don't want to talk about it anymore. My eyes flicker to the clock, seeing that it's nearly midnight. "But I think I'm gonna call it a night."

"Okay, well, like I said, consider the offer—and if you want to ensure there's nothing more to it, just *ask.*"

"Right, I know. Good night." I hang up the phone after she returns the good night, and I let out a sigh, making my way to the bedroom. Duke lazily follows me down the hall, and I close the door behind us, flipping the lock. It's a habit I've created any time Mason isn't here.

*The new norm now.*

I glance down at my phone, thankful he hasn't reached out again and plug it into the charger. Flipping back the covers, I crawl into bed as Duke settles in on the opposite side. And just as I close my eyes...

My phone vibrates against the nightstand.

# Six

## Henry

> Any thoughts on the deal?

I probably shouldn't have sent the message—I told myself I wouldn't—but as I lean against the log siding of the house, my eyes drift to the bedroom window, barely illuminated by the glow of a lamp or dimmed light.

*I know you read it, Lydia.*

My jaw tenses while I white knuckle my phone. I couldn't hear the phone conversation she was having a few minutes ago, and that was almost as frustrating as having to sit outside her house and *wait* for her to decide to take the deal of a lifetime.

The sound of my buzzing phone jars me, and I squint at the screen, biting down on my lip as I make out her name.

> I'm not sure I can agree to the terms. Your offer is very generous, but it seems like too much for the given work. I'm not sure it's right for me.

*Why are you being so hardheaded?* I let out a sharp breath as I type back, my mind filling with the images of breaking her window and taking her with me right now.

> I know you're the right person.

I smash the send button and then hesitate.

*That might've been too strong.*

I'm not used to giving anyone a choice. And while Lydia doesn't really have a choice, I'm trying to at least give her the illusion of one. I want her to fall for me...or *something*. I drum my fingers on the cold wood, waiting for her to reply.

But she doesn't.

My gaze shifts back to the window, and the light's gone. Lydia more than likely thinks she's going to mull it over for the night. *Do I have the patience for this?* I grind my teeth, the sound filling the void in my head.

I said I would take my time—but I didn't expect these complications. My nerves feel fried, and the risk I'm taking is stupid. Yet, here I am. My phone vibrates again, and I quickly lift it to my eyes. It's from Jude.

And it's a link to a new target.

*Fuck, no. Not right now.*

But that's not how my life works. When the links come, I have to go. My shoulders sag as I click on it, opening the new assignment.

*Location: Los Angeles.*

I nod to myself. No need to stress out. I text Jude back.

> Get intel. I'll take care of it when I get back.

> And when will that be?

> Tomorrow night.

Jude sends me a thumbs up, and I slide my phone into my pocket. It's time to see how secure Lydia's house is. I have no doubt the woman is packing. I'm well aware how southerners live their life. Admirable, really.

When they know how to use them.

I slip around to the front of the house. I saw her put the additional bar lock into the track of the back patio door earlier this evening. She's smart, I'll give her that. However, there are *three* entrances into this house, not including the windows. I'll make it through one of them. If I can't, I need to find a new profession. Lydia's front room light is off, and as I step onto the wooden porch, it creaks.

*We'll see how sharp you are, Duke.*

I listen carefully as I make my way to the door. Her lights aren't motion activated, so I'm still covered in the shadows of the porch. It makes for easy work. I reach for the doorknob—just in case I'm lucky enough to be let in. It's happened before.

You'd be surprised how many elitists leave their doors unlocked.

However, clearly, Lydia is not one of them. It doesn't budge. I slip my hand into my pocket, poking around for my lock picking tool. I had no intention of entering her house.

Playing it safe and all that.

But I just...I just need to take a quick peek. And my guess is that she's sleeping with the door closed, anyway. It's great for fires.

And terrible for hearing intruders.

I unlock the bottom lock and then move to the deadbolt. There're more efficient ways to unlock a deadbolt, but I don't want to ruin the lock. I need to leave this place untouched, and so after some tedious picking, I manage to unlock it.

*Too easy. It's too fucking easy.*

That's always what I think when I enter someone's house. They think it's their domain—that they're somehow safe by turning the locks on the doors at night. Sure, it might deter the petty, amateur guys.

But a true nightmare?

Yeah, we're gonna get in whether you lock up or not.

I turn the knob and push the door in slowly, relieved I don't have to deal with an additional chain lock. That would've added a few more minutes. The scent of warm vanilla and sandalwood smash into my senses, and somehow, it's welcoming. However, I highly doubt Lydia would be happy to see me here right now.

*Talk about a bad second impression. I should've brought the mask.*

But I don't have one tonight, and so I continue without it, taking in the usual mess of a house. She's not OCD when it comes to cleanliness, but the house isn't dirty. It's what I would expect out of a writer or left-brained person.

I've taken out a few.

My footsteps are dead quiet as I move through the small entry way into the living room. It's plain, but she has some sense of décor, considering the cabin-themed pictures hanging on the walls. Nothing expensive. Nothing extraordinary.

I wander over to the bookshelf, first scanning the pictures accentuating the books on the shelves. Most are of Duke and her family—or people I don't recognize. There's only one of her and Mason.

*Hate that.*

I grab it up, narrowing my eyes at the smiling faces. Lydia's appears strained, her lips tight, and Mason? Well, my guess is that he was probably drunk when the photo was taken. His eyes are slightly heavy, and he's leaning against her, his shoulders slumped. I frown.

She could do so much better.

Part of me wants to smash the frame into a million pieces and burn the photo—but that would probably wake up Lydia.

And that would be bad for all of us.

So, instead, I flip the frame over, unlatch the hooks and remove the picture. I put the empty frame back on the shelf. I tilt my head at the picture as I take it in one last time, and then rip it quietly right down the center, separating the two of them.

They don't belong together.

I shove the picture of Lydia into my pocket, only because I don't want to throw her in the trash. I do, however, wander over and drop Mason's picture in the trash after ripping him into a few more pieces.

Will she find it?

Probably. I kind of want her to.

I choose not to dwell on the thought and instead, take in the rest of the house. The kitchen is clean, dishes sitting neatly in the rack beside the sink. The kitchen table looks like it's never used, covered in books and other miscellaneous items. However, in front of one of the chairs there's a laptop.

And damn, I just can't help myself.

At first, I read the cute little bookish stickers on the cover. They're much more vanilla than I expected, but then again, some of the brightest lights are made with the darkest colors—or something like that. I open it, the bright light blinding as I click to unlock. I'm prepared to try and enter a passcode... But it doesn't ask for one.

*Come on, Lydia.*

My lips flatline as I shake my head. We'll go over her security later. I click through the windows she has open. The first one is a chapter outline, the next is a forty-thousand word partially written romantic comedy—*gross*—and the last is...

Our messages.

And that means she's been thinking about them.

*Or maybe that was just the last thing she did on the computer.*

I can't give myself too much credit. I've been irrevocably boring since I first reached out to her. I made it a point to be as mundane as possible in order to draw her into a normal business deal. She reacted much more strongly than I expected when we met—like she was downright terrified of me from the second she laid eyes on me.

*Fuck. Maybe this was a mistake.*

"Too late," I mutter inaudibly as I close the laptop. I give my eyes a second to adjust, and then head down the hallway. I pass a bathroom and two spare bedrooms, their doors wide open. One looks like some sort of study or office with shelving lining the walls and the second has a treadmill. As I reach the end of the hall, my heart rate kicks up a notch.

*There's a dog in there.*

The reminder keeps me on my toes as I peer at her door. If I reach out and turn that knob, and the dog wakes up to protect the house, I could be sent running. If I open the door and the dog remembers the protein bar in my pocket, I could also be left running. *If* I open the door, and the dog doesn't move, I'll get to view Lydia at one of her most vulnerable positions.

The risk is great, but damn, the reward is enticing.

I take a slow, steady breath as my fingers brush the doorknob. This isn't what I said I would do. I said I was going to play it safe, let her come to me, and here I am, on the brink of screwing it all up...

So I release the knob.

Talk about an exercise of patience.

# Seven

## Lydia

My eyes flutter open, the light streaming through the thin material of the curtains covering my bedroom window. Mason wanted blackout curtains, but I like waking up with the sunrise. As I roll over onto my side, Duke raises his head, his tail slapping the bed.

"Lemme guess," I begin, brushing my blonde hair from my face. "You need to go potty?"

He tilts his head and then jumps up, whining and shaking his butt at me. I blow out a sharp breath and sit up, the chill in the air causing my skin to prickle. I flip the covers back and grab my cardigan. After I pull it on, I pick up my phone from the nightstand.

> I know you're the right person.

I stare at the text as the chills run down my spine. I didn't reply to him last night, unsure of what to say. I've already made up my mind that I'm *not* going to California—I'm not going anywhere with him.

Duke whining at the door draws me out of my thoughts and I sigh, placing my phone in the pocket of my black sweater. I wrap it around my body tighter as I unlock and open the bedroom door.

I take a step forward and run right into the back of Duke. "What's wrong?" He *always* takes off like a jet down the hallway.

But not this morning.

He's standing stark still, his entire body rigid. And then he growls. I pedal backward, not stopping until I'm at my nightstand again. I pull open the drawer and retrieve my pistol. I rack it and return to Duke.

"Okay, let's go."

It's overkill. I know that. But with Duke's new habit of growling, I'm not taking any chances. I walk slowly down the hallway, hair bristling on the back of my neck.

But after a quick and thorough check, my house is empty.

Duke runs to the back door, whining more incessantly than ever.

I groan, feeling stupid for even freaking out. My house is locked up tight—and it always is. Not to mention, Duke would alert, right? He'd do more than growl. He'd bay, bark, or something.

*Maybe.*

He's never been in that kind of situation, but he didn't like Mason when he met him. In fact, he snapped at him twice over touching me. My dog would definitely attack someone with bad intentions. I set the gun on the kitchen counter and remove the bar in the track of the door, flip the lock, and slide it open, pulling the curtains with it.

Duke takes off at a sprint, and I follow him out, peering out into the morning. It's quieter than normal as Duke tears off into the woods. I try to follow him with my eyes, but I lose him in the thick brush.

And then he starts barking.

*What the hell?*

I squint out into the deep woods, trying to retrace where I had *just* watched him run—but I can't see him. I spin around and head back into the house, grabbing the pistol off the counter and returning to the deck.

Duke's barks grow more intense, and then shift to a snarl. I rush down the steps, my bare feet hitting the cold ground silently.

"Duke!" I take off toward the woods, more concerned that he's in a fight with a coyote or something. However, the closer I get, the more it sounds like it's coming from around the *front* of my house. I shift my direction and as I round the corner of the cabin, my heart stops at the sight. "What the hell are *you* doing here?"

Mason slams his truck door, glaring at Duke. "Call your stupid dog off, Lydia."

"No." I don't move, the gun still in my hand. "What're you doing here?"

The whites of his eyes are bloodred, and I figure either he's been crying, or he's spent the night out at the bars—and given that it's six-thirty in the morning, I'm guessing the latter.

"We need to talk," he growls, taking a step toward me.

Duke continues snarling, putting himself between the two of us. Honestly, I don't know why he's acting so aggressive toward Mason...

But I'm trusting him.

"You can come get your stuff when I'm not here."

"Like I have stuff here," Mason cackles. "You've been pushing me out for years now. It started out with me basically moving in, and then *you* thought I should get an apartment."

I take a step back, my stomach knotting up. "I needed the space."

"Because you wanted to fuck around."

*He's definitely been drinking.*

"I wanted you to make a decision about our relationship, and you chose to find an apartment instead of making up your mind." I'm white knuckling the gun, and I have no idea if he's even noticed I'm holding it.

"Yeah, right. Because everything always has to be done on *Lydia's* time."

"We'd been together for four and a half years," I say, keeping my voice as calm as I possibly can as he encroaches my space. "I just—"

"Don't play dumb," he snaps. "All you ever cared about is yourself. It's about *you* and *your* feelings all the time. You never asked me how I felt about anything at all."

I blink a couple of times. "I mean, I tried...You always said you didn't want to talk about it."

"Yeah, because I can't talk to you," he sneers. "You're just a pathetic, sad, moody woman who lives in her fucking head. And you know what? I only went out with you all those years ago because I was still messed up over Brit. I didn't even want to propose—but it's too late now. We're getting married. You don't get to decide this is over."

My stomach churns nauseously as I take a step back. "Please just leave."

He bursts into laughter. "What? You scared, Lydia? Isn't that what you like, though? Thought you'd like a man to rough you up." Mason's eyes darken as they rake over me. However, they pause as he realizes what's in my hand. "What're you doing with that?"

"I came to see what Duke was barking at..."

He snorts. "Go ahead and try to use that, Lydia. We all know you wouldn't have the fuckin' balls to pull the trigger."

"I have no intention of using it," I say, Duke still standing in front of me. "Please just go. You need to sober up or something."

"I'm not drunk," Mason shoots back at me. "Barely had anything. I just haven't been able to sleep because of *you*."

Duke lets out a loud bark as Mason takes another step toward me.

"Shut up!" he shouts at him, throwing his hands up. "I'll fucking punch your lights out."

"Don't," I warn as he raises his clenched fist.

Mason looks over at me and then chuckles. "Bet you'd shoot me over the dog. You've always loved him more than me."

I bite down on my lip, unsure of how to answer that. We both know it's true. But I don't want to do anything other than get Mason to *leave*.

"Let me have it." He extends his hand, his face feigning concern suddenly. "You look unstable, Lydia. Maybe we should look into getting you some therapy. You shouldn't have these kinds of fearful reactions to someone who loves you."

*Ah, there he goes.* It used to get to me and mess up my head, but it doesn't now. He can't gaslight me anymore.

"Leave now, please." As the words leave my lips, my phone begins to ring in my pocket.

"Who is that?" Mason demands, gesturing to my cardigan pocket. "I don't—"

"*Look.*"

Keeping my eye on him, I pull it out, my heart skipping as I see Henry's name on the screen. *Why is he calling me at this time in the morning? Did I turn on the read receipts on accident?*

"Who is it?" Mason nearly shouts.

"Spam," I answer him, keeping my voice flat.

"Right," he scoffs. "I bet."

I've backed up enough now that I have a clear view of the back door. My heart pounds in my head, anxiety and fear racking my body. I should have the upper hand with the dog and gun, but Mason seems on the verge of losing it.

But I could probably make it to the door. My phone rings again.

Mason's face grows red. "*Who is calling you?!*"

I look up from the screen just as Mason lunges at me. He almost is able to secure my arm, but Duke pounces at the same time. His teeth don't connect fully but do tear Mason's jacket sleeve. I raise the gun, firing off one shot into the ground near his feet.

And then I run like hell.

"You crazy bitch!" Mason screams from somewhere behind me. "You just tried to shoot me!"

But I don't look behind me, not even as Duke joins me. I fly up the back porch steps, and through the back patio door, slamming it shut. I flip the lock and then grab the bar, securing it. I can barely breathe as I begin to pace my living room, terrified.

"I'm calling the fucking cops!" Mason shouts from somewhere outside. "You're a psycho bitch!"

A few tense minutes pass. I can't see him, but I know he's still out there—I'd hear his truck if he left. But then again, I didn't hear him pull up. My hands tremble as I pull my phone from my pocket, seeing the two missed calls from Henry.

*What could he possibly want right now?*

I ignore them, trying to decide what the hell I'm supposed to do. I shouldn't have fired the gun. I could've hit him. I mean, I'm a good shot, but still. He could get me for attempted murder or something.

I don't wanna go to jail.

Tears well up in my eyes as my entire body begins to shake. I run to the front windows, peering out into the yard. Mason's climbing into his truck. He's leaving.

*I'm so screwed.*

But it's my word against his, right? I mean, would they be able to tell I even shot at the ground? And he was trespassing, so that counts for something.

My phone pings with a message from him.

> You'll pay for this.

I don't reply. Instead, I rub my arms violently. His text is a threat, so that has to count for something, too, if the police come knocking.

*Or maybe I should call them to get ahead of this.*

A sob breaks loose in my chest as Mason drives away, slinging gravel and spinning his tires. I go back to the living room and climb onto the couch, curling my knees to my chest. Duke joins me as I drop my head, letting my cries rock me.

And I stay like that for a while. Until my stupid phone pings again.

I lift my head, using my sleeve to wipe the tears from my cheeks. Nervously, I dig it out of my pocket and stare at the message from Emma.

> Have you made a decision about the contract?

I sigh, knowing I have to do something about Henry. It's not professional to leave him waiting—the man flew in just to meet me for the job. I swallow hard, wondering if I should call him or text him...

Maybe I *could* work something out with him. I could write it from a distance, and then I wouldn't have to deal with the way he intimidates me.

It's worth a shot.

I might need the money for a freaking lawyer, anyway. I navigate to the text thread and type out a message.

> I might be willing to take the job if you're open to discussing some of the terms.

Three dots appear immediately.

> Sure. I'd prefer to discuss them in person. It's easier than texting.

I let out a sharp breath. *Of course, he wants to discuss them in person. Why not torture me a little more?* But then again, it would get me out of the house and away from Mason for a while.

> I'll meet you at the coffee shop in an hour and a half.

That's plenty of time for me to get ready and make it to the city. I'll call Emma or my mom on the way. Someone needs to know what happened this morning.

> Give me three hours.

I frown. What could he possibly have to do this morning? I push the thought away. It doesn't matter. I send him a quick reply and then leave my phone on the coffee table. Regardless of Henry being busy, I won't be hanging around here. I can find something to do away from the house.

And I'll take Duke, too.

Just in case Mason comes creeping around the house again.

# Eight

## Henry

*What are you doing, Mason?*

I sigh, watching his truck as he turns around at the highway and heads *back* toward Lydia's house. He's already signed his death warrant with that stunt he pulled earlier, which is why I left Lydia's to follow the prick. Before he even lunged at Lydia, I knew something would have to be done with him, but he just made the decision much easier. Lydia is no longer his to touch—or berate, for that matter.

As much as I was rooting for Lydia to shoot the fucker, I'm glad I get to be the one who takes care of him. It would've been a shame to have to drop in and surprise her anyway. There'd have been no way to explain myself.

Of course, me calling her in the middle could've led her to assume things. However, I don't think it did. I don't think she thought about it at all—though I do know she checked her phone in the middle of their tense conversation.

My thoughts are drawn back as Mason's truck speeds up.

*I'll have to stop him close to her house. Really close.*

And that's inconvenient. It'll put me right out in the open, which is never good a place to be. But the risk is worth the peace it'll bring Lydia. I smash the gas on the Tahoe and fly by Lydia's house, hoping that she's too traumatized to look out the window. I unclick my seatbelt and grab my handgun from the console. Glancing up at my new target, I know this might get a little loud.

And based on the speed Mason's travelling, he's still very pissed off.

I just hope he's sober enough to hit the brakes in time. I jerk the wheel of the Tahoe, and park across the gravel road, preventing Mason from going around me. There're thick woods on both sides, leaving little to no shoulder. It's a good spot to block him.

Mason's truck skids to a stop as his hands fly up in the air. He's irate now, slinging open the driver's side door. I count to five in my head, take a deep breath, and open my door. The Tahoe separates us, but it won't for long. This guy is on a fucking rampage...

But he has no idea who he's up against.

Mason, his dress shirt unbuttoned about halfway down, comes stalking toward me. "What the fuck is wrong with you? You can't just block the road. Move your mom car out of the way."

"Sorry, man," I say, climbing out and shrugging. "Car trouble."

Mason stares at me for a few beats, his eyes narrowing. "Hard to believe when I just saw you park there. And you know what? I've never seen you around here before either. You don't live on this road—and it's a dead end. So what the hell are you doing?"

"Aw," I glance around us, frowning. "Guess I got a little turned around."

Mason lingers there, studying me. His eyes are bloodshot, and he reeks of a bar. "You were with Lydia, weren't you?"

*Wow, jumping to some big conclusions.*

"I'm sorry, who? Are you okay?" I almost laugh, his face reddening.

"Who the hell are you?" He steps forward, nearing the edge of my personal space. "Her side piece?"

Okay, now I'm laughing.

"What the *fuck* is so funny?" he roars, lunging at me similarly to how he did Lydia. Mason's not agile, given the drinks and the fatigue. I dip and raise the butt of my gun, nailing him right in the occipital nerve on the back of his head. His body goes limp, and I catch him, whipping open the backseat and shoving him inside.

He won't be out for long, so I quickly zip-tie his wrists and ankles and then slam the door. Now I have to get rid of the loser's truck.

*What a pain in the ass.*

I blow out a breath and head for Mason's vehicle. It reeks of cigarette smoke inside, and one look around tells me he's been drinking...a *lot.* There're crushed beer cans on the floorboard, along with an open one in the cupholder.

"This is a little much, Mason," I mutter, slamming the driver's side door shut. I have two options for this truck. I can risk driving past Lydia's to that abandoned trailer...Or I can risk driving around looking for a place to stash it until I can get a crew here to do my dirty work.

I run my tongue along my bottom lip. *Never mind.* I see a third choice. There's no fence along the shoulder, only brush. It's not the best decision, but I stomp the gas, and send the truck through it. This *might* leave evidence that's not on our side, but...

It'll be fine. I've done worse.

I shift it to four-wheel-drive and run deeper into the woods, careful not to bust the radiator or anything stupid like that. I'm already gonna hear about this, but I'll enjoy it all first. I cut the engine once

I know I'm deep enough it won't catch any obvious attention. I can have a crew here overnight.

*As long as Lydia doesn't turn me down again.*

Damnit. That could complicate things. I don't give it much thought though, slipping out and heading back toward the road. I didn't think it all the way through when I left the Tahoe parked across the road. If Lydia decides to leave, this could be a problem.

But as I step out of the thick woods, the road is clear. I head back to my rental, pausing to see what the entrance looks like. I give myself an approving nod. That fixes that. You can't even tell anything has been driven into the woods. The stemmy trees popped right back up from where I had mowed them over.

*Now to deal with this dipshit.*

Rage and excitement flood my system as I climb into the driver's seat and peek back at Mason. He's still passed out, which is much to my benefit. I don't want to listen to his mouth while I move him. I drive past Lydia's house, unbothered this time. The hard part is done.

I glance down at my watch.

*Fifty-five minutes to finish.*

So much for having too much fun. I turn down the grass covered road, making my way back to the trailer, parking just out front.

*Well, here we go.*

Ten minutes later, he's tied off to a chair in the middle of the abandoned kitchen. It's really a benefit for me that the old lady left her furniture. It's like everything here is meant to be, falling into place like fate.

If you believe in such a notion.

I lean against the kitchen bar, taking in the drabby components of the mobile home. It hasn't been updated since the nineties, but I have to give it to the lady, she kept the place clean. It's just dusty from no one living here.

Well, and it smells like a nursing home and death, but I've smelled worse.

"What the fuck." A groan grabs my attention. "Where am I?"

"Ah, you're awake." I keep my arms folded across my chest.

"Who *are* you?" Mason lifts his head, looking up at me wearily. He doesn't have much fight in him, which isn't all that surprising.

I let out a sigh. "I guess I could introduce myself." I stick out my hand. "Henry Bayne."

Recognition flashes across Mason's face, but I don't think he actually connects the dots. His eyes drop to his bindings as he squirms. "What the..."

"Oh right." I take my hand back, laughing. "You're a little restrained."

He makes a weird face at me, his lip curling upward in disgust. "What the fuck is wrong with you?"

"More like what *isn't* wrong with me," I say dryly. "But anyway, I'm pressed for time, and as much as I'd love to draw out this conversation, I have a meeting to get to before my flight leaves this evening. I had imagined something more intricate, but this'll do."

His eyes widen as I pull out my blade. "Wh-what are you doing, bro? Is this over me gettin' a little pissed about the road? It's not a big deal. Just call it water under the bridge—"

"You're a bloody idiot," I snap, shaking my head at him. "You really think I would slit someone's throat over a little road rage?"

*I mean, maybe. I don't know.*

"Then what the hell is this?"

"You tried to put your hands on something that belongs to me, and that's punishable by death, I'm afraid."

"I have no idea what you're talking about."

"I believe you read over the contract I provided your fiancée." I hate using that word when it comes to Lydia and another man, but the reference finally hits this motherfucker.

"Whoa..." His voice trails off as he looks up at me. "*You're* the dude that flew all the way here for some stupid book?"

I frown. "It's unbecoming to talk about someone's work in that manner."

"It's just a book."

"Have you ever read one?"

"A book? Of course, I have. I'm not an imbecile."

*That's debatable.*

"I meant one of *hers*."

"Uh, no, but she knows it's not my thing. I don't like to read that weird shit she writes, but..." His face flashes with understanding. "I bet *you* do. You probably get off to the dirty scenes."

"I can be a sicko," I admit, running the tip of my finger along the blade edge. I don't press hard enough to break skin, but the hard swallow from Mason makes me smile. "But to tell you the truth, I have read her works."

"And what? You're some psycho fan who beats off to my girl's picture?"

My face twists up in disgust. "I'm not a pervert, Mason, though psycho might be fitting."

"But you're willing to pay her all that money for a book? Or are you wanting to fuck her, too for that?"

"You're shallow enough to put a price on her, I see," I comment, taking a step toward Mason. His body trembles, and I'm not sure if it's the lack of heat or the fear I see wafting up from him.

"People pay for sex all the time."

"I wasn't paying her for sex. I was paying her to write a book."

"But you intended to fuck her."

"You should've been a lawyer," I run the tip of my blade down the curve of his jaw, slicing just enough that it begins to bleed.

And Mason wails like a dying rabbit.

*Jeez. Excessive.*

I crack my neck to the side, placing the edge of the blade just beneath his ear.

"No, don't," he cries, his voice breaking into a whine.

"Come on, Mason. It's just a cut. We both know you would've done worse to Lydia had you been able to get your hands on her."

"No, I wouldn't have."

"Yeah, I saw it in your eyes." That's the truth, too. He had that look of desperation and rage. It's a deadly combination and becomes heightened when a control freak loses his ability to control. Lydia stripped him of that, and I wouldn't have been surprised if he'd have wrapped his hand around her pretty neck...

But that's my spot.

"Okay, fine," Mason's voice darkens.

I dig the blade in a little deeper, breaking skin. "*Okay, fine,* what?"

"I was gonna rough her up a little. Sometimes women just need to be put in their place. It's not the first time—"

*Nope.*

The ringing in my ears drowns out his screams as I drag the blade across his skin, my own rage flooding my senses. Blood spews everywhere, covering me, but I still finish the job, having nearly decapitated him with the force of my anger. It's always a doozy when that carotid gets sliced.

I then step back, admiring the sight as he hangs there limp in the chair. Blood pools on the floor beneath his feet, droplets still raining down silently from his neck. I wish there'd have been more time. I'd have loved to have had the chance to crush every bone in his body, chop his dick right off...

But it is what it is.

*He won't touch you again, Lydia.*

An alarm goes off on my watch, and I realize it's time for me to go. I'll call the clean-up crew and wash up at the hotel before I meet her. I'll have to be quick.

Because I'd really fucking hate to be late.

# Nine

## Lydia

I stare at my phone resting on the table of the coffee shop. It's five minutes until ten o'clock, and for some reason, I'm starting to wonder if he's even going to show up—would I even care?

I can't make up my mind.

I don't really know Henry, but ever since meeting him in person yesterday, I haven't been able to shake him.

*I'll just tell him it's not going to work.*

It's as though I'm breaking up with someone all over again, and I inwardly cringe at the thought. And speaking of that, I haven't heard from Mason since he left my house. And even as much as I *should* have told someone what happened, I haven't had the nerve to do it.

*They're all just going to think I'm crazy.*

I mean, I shot at him—well, not at him—but in the vicinity of his feet. I think that still counts as *at him* though. *Am* I going nuts? And since when do I even do shit like this? I'm not confrontational. Did Henry flip some kind of weird switch in me?

*No, that's impossible. Fifteen minutes with someone doesn't do that.*

My forehead rests against the palm of my hand as I start to spiral again, replaying the scene with Mason as a distraction from Henry. I think he could have me charged, but would Mason do that? Maybe he'll just sleep it off and let it go...

*Or he'll show back up to my house.*

That makes me shudder. Mason has never put his hands on me. Well, not really. The worst he's done is shouting in my face, and he's also thrown things in my general direction. However, he did lunge to grab me this morning...

And the expression on his face was unnerving.

"No coffee?" a voice cuts into my thoughts.

A chill runs down my spine. I force my eyes upward, taking in the god of a man standing above me. I swallow hard at the icy eyes looming over me.

*Why is he so attractive, and yet so freaking intimidating?*

He cocks a brow at me when I just stare at him in silence. "Okay..."

"Sorry," I rip my eyes from his, my gaze falling to my hands. "It's been a long day."

"The day just started," he chuckles, sliding into the seat across from me. His tone is so light, so indifferent, and I peek up at him, studying the strong structures of his face. His elongated, masculine nose, his strong jaw line, and his perfectly proportioned lips are the most prominent, but there's also something about his aura that feels like a tantalizing *spell* might have been cast on me.

He's like the pied piper, drawing me in just to lead me to my death or something.

I swallow hard and try to shake it off. It's crazy talk. "I'm sorry."

"Why are you apologizing?" he counters, leaning back in the chair. We're in a public place, but we might as well be alone. I can't process anything in front of me other than this man...

And it's a legit reminder of *why* this is a huge no.

"I don't think it'll work," I blurt out, clasping my hands in my lap. "I don't think it's a good time for me to relocate."

"Why's that?" He makes this face like he thinks I'm full of shit—and I definitely am when it comes to my excuses.

"I have a dog," I say stupidly.

"You can bring him."

"You like dogs?"

"If they're yours, I suppose."

My heart flutters at his words, even if I have no idea how to take them—but I can't let him sway me. So, I shake my head.

"I don't understand." His voice drops a notch. "If you'd like more compensation for the book, we can discuss that."

My eyes widen. "It's not about the compensation. In fact, I'd be fine with *less* compensation and I'll write the book from here."

His eyes narrow and he leans forward, giving me a strong whiff of his musky cologne. "Are you scared to leave this shithole?"

Well, now I'm offended.

He smirks. "You have a soft spot for this place—or have you just never left?"

*Both.*

I shift in my seat, gathering my last bit of courage. "I don't think it really matters my reasonings. I would just prefer not to move in with a stranger for the duration of the job."

His upper lip twitches in a way that makes my stomach knot up. Henry takes a long, deep breath. And if I didn't know better, I would think what I said annoyed him.

"I just don't feel comfortable with the arrangement," I explain further, trying that whole *honesty is the best policy* belief.

He nods curtly. "So, what *would* make you comfortable, Lydia?"

I stare at his mouth, my name sounding like heaven coming from it.

And he chuckles.

"What?" I blink a few times, heat flushing to my cheeks.

He runs a finger across the top of the table and sighs. "You seem like you're struggling to keep your thoughts in order today. You sure you're okay?"

"Yeah." My gaze flicks up to his eyes, and the amusement is nearly more than my heart can take. Those grayish blue irises dance across my face like a flame, leaving my skin feeling hot.

*What would it be like if he actually touched me?*

I play with the idea. I *am* single now. Nothing is stopping me from making terrible decisions. He's frightening, yeah, but there's just something about him that makes me want to test those dark waters.

"What would make you comfortable?" he repeats himself, this time his words sharpening.

Blinking a few times, I push away the thoughts of his hands on my body. "I already told you. I'd rather work on the project remotely. I rarely travel for the books I write—and when I do, it's not with my client."

He purses his lips. "I can't bend to that. I'm more than happy to up the compensation and accept your dog, but I can't let you work on the project remotely."

My shoulders fall. "Then I can't do the project."

*And I don't want to, anyway.*

The muscles in Henry's jaw grow taught and his eyes dart from mine, shifting to the exit of the coffee shop. I can't tell if he's going to jump up and leave, or if mentally, he's tearing me to shreds over this rejection. Either seems plausible—or maybe both. I don't know, but the tense moment has my hair standing on end.

"I'm sorry to put you out," I begin, the people pleaser in me showing its hand. "I'm more than happy to compensate you for your time and travelling."

*If I can afford it.*

He laughs sardonically and dark, shaking his head. "I don't need your reimbursement, Lydia."

*Well, okay then.*

I swallow hard and look away, my face flushing with heat. I'm the kind of woman who used to cry when I got embarrassed—and this is one of those times, a lump beginning to form in my throat. Thankfully, after years of being with Mason, I've learned how to deal with it. I count to ten in my head, focusing on anything but the demeaning laughter coming from Henry.

And then, I replace the embarrassment with anger.

"This meeting is over," I level with him, challenging that mind numbing gaze of his. "I think it's clear we can't agree on this."

His expression darkens as his tongue runs along his bottom lip. "You'll regret this, Lydia. It's a once in a lifetime opportunity."

"Maybe, but I'm not changing my mind." I slip my hand into my bag and pull out the contract. "I'm certain you can find someone else who will agree to your terms. I'm not the most talented nor the most proficient. For this kind of money, it should be easy to find just about anyone." I slide it across the table to him, but his eyes remain on my face. "Again, I'm sorry for wasting your time." As I go to stand, he finally responds, his voice low and severe.

"And you're sure this is what you want to do?"

I pause, my heart thumping in my chest like a hammer to my ribcage. "Yes, *Henry*. I'm sure."

His eyes flicker with something undiscernible. "The offer will remain on the table if you change your mind."

I sling my bag over my shoulder. "I'm not changing my mind. I already said that."

"Mmm" is all he says, pulling his eyes from mine.

"Have a good rest of your day and have a safe flight home." I start for the door, bracing for him to reach out and grab me, stopping me from leaving.

But he doesn't.

He lets me go, and a few minutes later, I'm greeting Duke, who was sleeping in the backseat of my SUV the entire duration of the meeting.

"Maybe I read too much into him," I mumble to Duke but mostly to myself as I peer into the coffee shop. Henry's not chasing me out or blowing up my phone. In fact, as I sit there in my car, staring through the coffee shop windows, I see him walk to the counter and order a coffee, giving the barista a warm smile.

*He never smiles like that at me.*

A pang of jealousy hits me, and I shake my head. *How stupid.* Everything about him feels dangerous. There's nothing to be jealous of. I'm probably dodging a bullet...

And I have enough on my plate as it is.

I don't think I can take on someone as intense as Henry... and not lose my mind.

# Ten

## Henry

*This is a fucking mess.*

Lydia should have said yes. Why the hell did she *not* say yes? She's still under the assumption her arrogant dipshit of an ex is still living and breathing. Why would she stay with the creep lurking around? Is she just trying to be brave? Stubborn?

What. The. Fuck.

My jaw is cramping from how tense it's been since she left. I didn't follow her out, because if I did, I know I would've shoved her and her dog into my car and taken her against her will.

But I don't want that.

I want to lie my way into her heart and mind, consume her, and then break her with the truth when I think she can handle the repair of what I've done. I'm a fucking snake, is what I am.

And she *will* accept that. Eventually.

My fingers grip the edge of the table as I stand to my feet. Lydia's probably almost home by now, but I didn't chase her, because I know she's safe. Mason is nothing but a pile of ashes by now. The only person she has to fear is right here.

And damn, if the dark monster in me isn't trying to rear its ugly head. Lydia clearly needs some encouragement to change her mind and make the right decision.

*Let the games begin.*

I grab the contract she left on the table and shove it into my backpack. Part of me would like to show up and shove it down her throat for having the audacity to hand it back—but that's not the right thing to do. I know that.

My phone vibrates in my pocket as I exit the coffee shop, my mind trying to formulate the next move. I don't have a lot of time before the assignment will come due, and the Big Man doesn't like it when we accept a hit and run late.

I squint across the parking lot as I walk. It's overcast and gloomy outside. Quite fitting for how defeated and enraged I'm feeling in the moment. The black Tahoe stands out like a sore thumb, covered in a white dust from the gravel roads I've been frequenting—and will continue to frequent.

*Guess I need to extend the rental.*

I slide into the driver's seat and only then do I retrieve my phone from my jacket pocket. I open the message from one of my cleanup crew contacts. The mess I made is taken care of, and the truck is off to a chop shop.

Brilliant. Now Jude will just have to take care of the digital details. But besides that, everything is ready for our departure.

"Well, except *her*." I scroll to Jude's number and hit the call button as I pull out of the parking lot. It feels a lot like de ja vu right now. *Agonizing* de ja vu. Back to Lydia's I go.

Three rings in, Jude growls over the speakers. "What the hell did you do?"

"Nice to hear from you, too," I say flatly.

"I just got the invoice for a cleanup—and there was a *vehicle disposal?* Please tell me you didn't kill the woman."

"Of course, I didn't," I snap. "You know I don't do that."

"Yeah, I didn't think you *stalked* and *seduced* women either, yet here we are, and now you're apparently mixing some murder—"

"He had it coming."

"Of course, he did," Jude scoffs. "Save me the details."

"I need you to create a digital footprint for Mason Prewitt. He needs to quit his job, move away—something. You know the drill."

He sighs. "The fiancé. You killed the fiancé."

"Ex-fiancé," I correct him.

"So if he was the *ex*, why did you bother? Seems like a waste of time."

I white knuckle the steering wheel. "Just do what I asked you to."

"You know I will."

My eyes take in the empty turnpike, and for a moment, I actually appreciate the middle of nowhere. No bumper-to- bumper traffic. "Also, I need you to cancel my flight and extend the rental."

Silence.

"Jude?"

"You *have* to get back here."

*Fuck.*

"I can't. I'm not going without her."

"Yeah, you are. Can you imagine what the Big Man is going to do if we're late? The longer you put it off, the closer we get to being on his radar—and if he finds out about what you're doing out there..."

"We work off contracts. It's none of his business what we do outside of them."

"Yeah, till he finds out *that's* the reason why you're not here. I accepted the job, Henry. We have to do it."

"And I will do it. I'm just not going without Lydia."

"Oh jeez," he groans. "You can't be serious. Maybe I should call Cher. She'd be thrilled to know that you're off stalking her favorite author and trying to kidnap her."

Irritation burns in my chest, rivalling the guilt her name brings up. "Don't hold my sister over my head. I'm not going to kidnap Lydia. Just scare her into taking the deal."

"This could go *so* bad."

"It could, and then I'll do whatever I have to. She has no idea her ex-fiancé is gone, so I can use that to my advantage. I know how to drive people out."

"You're a lunatic, but you're right." He sighs heavily on the other end of the line. "Just...Be careful. Please. If something happens to you out there, I'll have to call Luca, and you know how I feel about that."

I frown, thinking of our friend, one which makes the monster in me look like an angel. "Yeah, no need to get him involved. Ever."

"It would tickle his fancy to know you're out playing dangerous games, though."

"I'm sure it would, but no one needs to know about this."

"Never would've told anyone, anyway. You still have eight hours to make the flight, you know."

I glance at the clock. "No, it's going to have to wait. I need the cover of dark. I can't have her recognizing me."

"Yeah, fair enough. Let me know as soon as you have something, though. Hopefully sooner rather than later."

*Hopefully.*

\*\*\*

She's spent the entire day locked inside her house. I mean, Lydia literally hasn't stepped one foot outside. She only slides the door open enough to let the dog out—and then closes it immediately. Her paranoia has gone up a few notches. And as I sit there, crouched in the cover of the thick woods, I ready myself. She's going to bed soon...

And it's time to get started.

She'll probably call the police, but I can handle that. I've never done this sort of thing with a woman, but I've taken it upon myself to terrify plenty of my targets before taking care of them. I didn't get that opportunity with Mason, unfortunately.

I glance down at the white mask with x's over the eyes. I have only one concern when it comes to this whole plan—her shooting at me.

But I intend to fix this problem tonight.

I wait for the lights to turn off in the house and sit for another hour and a half. It's a grueling wait, but I do what I have to do. And then I jump to my feet and make my way to the front door.

It's the easiest access point, and I slip into the entry way just like before. I fix the mask, dog treat in hand. I have to get into Lydia's room tonight...

And my mind runs rampant with what I *could* do while I'm there. My body reacts, but I push the thought away.

*Nope.*

Tonight, my hands will be full...*of guns.*

I pour over the kitchen and living room, searching for any weapons that she might've hid around the house. It's not uncommon for paranoid people to have guns stashed all over the place. However, as I make my way down the hallway, my hands are empty. I slip into the first spare room and check there, but again, empty.

The second room gives me more hope as I spot the gun safe in the corner.

Lucky for me, it's a keypad.

I pull out my light, seeing what keys have been pressed the most before I get tricky—and as they illuminate, it doesn't take an idiot to realize it's her birthday.

*Not a smart move, Lydia.*

The safe is open within seconds, and I creep through the contents while removing the twelve-gauge shotgun, .223 hunting rifle, a 9mm pistol, and all the ammunition in sight. I set them to the side quietly, keeping my ear in tune for the dog. I have a treat in my pocket, laced with a sedative. I've done it with animals before if they forget we're friends. However, it does me absolutely no good if they get a step ahead of me.

Thankfully, I pick up nothing in the air, and fish through the contents of the massive safe. My fingers land on a white envelope, and I pull it out, sifting through the cash. It's a couple thousand. I put it back, and continue, looking for anything I don't already have on file. Most of it is useless, consisting of warranties for appliances, insurance policy documents, and other random financial papers.

It's disappointing, really.

I close the safe door and gather up the guns and ammunition. I slip back through the house and out the front door, stacking them just inside of the woods. If I have to leave quickly, I don't need to be trying to grab my arm full of weapons. I dust my hands off, and head back into the house, my heart beating more rapidly as I make my way to her room.

*How light of a sleeper are you, Lydia?*

I swallow hard, carefully checking the doorknob. It's locked, naturally. I peer down at the mechanism and then nearly laugh. Locks like these are a joke. I dig into my pocket and pull out a small blade, inserting it like a flat head into the slit.

And then I twist until it clicks.

*Here we go.*

My fingers grasp the brass knob and I turn it silently. If the door squeaks, I'll be screwed with the dog. Duke isn't exactly a protection animal, but he's more aware than the smaller types of dogs I've dealt with.

Though the yappy ones always pose a problem.

I push the door inward, holding my breath beneath the mask. I take in the blackness of the room. For some reason, I expected there to be a night light or something, but obviously, Lydia prefers pitch black. I blink my eyes to adjust, spotting Duke sleeping soundly on the bed. I reach up and lift the mask, pulling out the treat.

I have to take care of him first.

My footsteps are silent as I make my way around the bed. And he finally hears me from the deep sleep he was in. "Easy," I whisper, holding out the treat. His tail slaps the bed as he takes it from my hand. "Good boy." I pat his head, my heart rate coming down a few notches. I can relax a little. My eyes flicker to Lydia, curled up on her side and facing the dog.

*Wow. She looks peaceful.*

I pause to admire her, and the monster in me pulls at the urges washing through my body. Every ounce of my being wants to pull those covers back, spread her legs, and take her. *Fuck consent. Fuck this patience.*

My lips flatline. It would be *so* easy. Would she scream? Would she know it was me? I adjust my jeans and rip my eyes from her. As tempting as it is, I keep the lustful monster on his tight chain. Besides, I have a job to do tonight.

I distract myself with scouring her room for weapons.

And the search does not disappoint. The woman really loves shotguns, apparently, which is as much of a turn-on as it is concerning. I slide out a ten-gauge from under her bed along with a set of hunting knives. This woman is the epitome of a country woman, I think. I set them over by the door as Duke finishes his treat and drifts off to sleep.

I make my way to Lydia's side of the bed. I'm still missing the gun she tried to shoot Mason with, and I *know* it's going to be close to her. I squint in the darkness and see the steel barrel resting on the nightstand beside her.

This is the one that will make the biggest impact. When she wakes up, she'll know immediately it's gone. And that's exactly what I need. Maybe she'll call the cops. Maybe she'll point the finger at Mason.

After all, she *did* shoot at him.

I take one more look at her, her blonde hair spilled over the burgundy pillow. My breath catches. Someday, she's going to let me into her bed. In fact, she's going to beg for it. We're just not there yet.

But we'll get there.

*Goodnight, Lydia.*

# Eleven

## Lydia

I shoot up in my bed, my body trembling. If I had a nightmare, I don't remember it. My head whips around to Duke, sleeping peacefully beside me. A shiver runs down my spine. It's not even daylight yet. My eyes drift to the clock projecting on the wall.

*4:57 a.m.*

My hand flies to my eyes, rubbing the sleep from them. It's early, but not *that* early. I flip back the covers, jitters still creeping down my arms. I reach for my phone, picking it up from the nightstand...

And then I freeze.

*Where's my gun?*

Did it fall off? I peer over the edge of the bed at the hardwood floor. There's nothing there. I slide off and drop to my knees, reaching under blindly and checking between the nightstand and my bed frame.

*Nothing.*

My heart starts to race as I lower my head to get a more thorough view.

*Where's my shotgun?*

Now I'm about to panic. I know it was there last night. I double-checked. I made *sure,* considering the moment I stepped through my door, I started panicking about Mason showing back up unannounced. I nearly run to the other side of my bed, going for my set of hunting knives before I go creeping through the house.

But they're gone, too.

What. The. Hell.

I reach for Duke, shaking him slightly. "Duke, wake up." My heart sinks when he doesn't instantly respond. However, a few moments later, he lifts his head, peering up at me with sleepy eyes. He slowly climbs to his feet before stretching his front paws forward, letting out a loud yawn.

"Come on," I tell him, my hands shaking as I go for my bedroom door. It's unlocked. A sob jars my chest as I touch the knob, terrified of what might be on the other side. I turn it slowly, pull the door inward, and brace.

But there's no one there.

And Duke races happily for the backdoor like he does every morning. In fact, he might be a little *more* excited than usual. My body trembles as I white knuckle my phone, stepping into the hallway. However, instead of joining Duke at the door, I step into the office, heading straight for the gun safe. I'm not walking through this freaking house without *something*.

I peer around me, but the room is quiet, the only sound being my fingers punching in the code. The lock clicks and I open the safe.

And then gasp.

Tears slip down my cheeks as panic fills my chest. There's only one person who knows the code to my safe.

*Mason.*

My mouth grows dry as I pull my phone out, dialing 9-1-1. However, before I hit the call button, I rethink the move. Is that who I should call? Or just the sheriff's office? I don't want to interfere with real emergencies. Is this a real emergency? My finger smashes the call button.

Forget it. I'm not leaving this room until someone comes to help me.

***

Fifteen minutes later, I'm racing to the front door, whipping it open to greet the sheriff's deputy. Duke stands behind me, peering around my legs. He's still yet to be let out to use the bathroom and seems a little out of it this morning. Is he sick? Or am I just overanalyzing it?

"Lydia Waters?"

I nod, tightening the robe around me as I choke out, "Yes."

"I'm Deputy Briggins. Is there any signs of someone still being in here?" The deputy is a good ten years older than me—and he does not look enthused to be here. I gaze out into the yard, worry probing my brain. Will he even care?

I shake my head. "No, but I locked myself in the spare room until you got here."

He sighs. "Do I have permission to check the residence?"

I bob my head and step out of the way, letting the heavyset officer slip past me. I wait by the entryway as he draws his gun and checks every nook and cranny.

He returns to me, holstering his gun. "Inside is clear. I can check around outside. You said your guns are missing?"

"Yeah, they emptied my safe, too."

"Any other valuables missing?"

I blink a couple of times. "I don't...I don't know."

He raises a brow at me. "Maybe you should check?"

"Um, yeah, of course." I take off for the gun safe, knowing there's a stash of cash tucked away in the back corner. Mason had no clue it was there, but if he saw it...I know he would've taken it. Deputy Briggins follows me to the spare room, and I reopen the safe, reaching for the white letter-sized envelope.

Still there.

I pour over the rest of the contents. "Nothing else is missing."

"Well, I guess we'll just write up a report for the guns."

"Is that it?" I gape. "I mean, someone broke into my house last night and stole the pistol right off my nightstand."

"Why did you have a gun on your nightstand?"

*Shit.*

"My ex-fiancé hasn't taken our split very well." *And I shot at him.* But I don't mention that. However, the realization hits me like a ton of bricks. I might be digging my own grave with this report...But what else am I supposed to do? My stomach churns.

"I see. And so, he came and stole your guns?" Deputy Briggins studies my face. "Has anything else happened?"

"Um." I hesitate, hung on whether or not to tell the deputy the truth.

"If something has occurred between the two of you, it's better for me to know now, than to find out later." His voice is indifferent, almost robotic.

"He showed up at my house unannounced and drunk. He lunged at me." I leave out the part where I shot at him again, though I know Mason won't. I need to call a lawyer or something.

"I see, and did you feel threatened?" "Yes," I snap at him.

"Why didn't you call it in then?"

"I don't know. He left. I thought I was fine."

"Who is your ex-fiancé?"

"Mason Prewitt."

Recognition flashes across his face. "Seriously? Like Jim and Karen's Mason Prewitt?"

*Shit. He knows him.*

"Yeah, that's him."

"Huh, okay. Well, I'll take the report. How many guns went missing? You got the paperwork on them?"

I gather the necessary documentation and hand it over to Deputy Briggins, who seems to relax after finding out I assume it was Mason. He gives me a nod and heads toward the front door, Duke padding along quietly. I glance down at him, still a little suspicious of the way he's behaving. He never likes strangers.

"Are you going to check around outside?" I ask the deputy as he steps out onto my front porch.

He glances around, his beady brown eyes making a quick scan. "You sure Mason's not just playing a joke on you? Or maybe you just don't remember him picking up the guns? Did any of them belong to him?"

*You have to be freaking kidding me.*

"No, they all belonged to me. And no, I don't think it's a joke."

He shrugs. "Okay, well, maybe consider changing your locks. I'll look into this."

As I watch him head off the porch, making his way to his car, a terrible feeling rolls over my body, and I'm fairly certain of one thing...

He's *not* going to be looking into it.

I watch the car leave the driveway, and let Duke slip out to go to the bathroom. I stand there in the open doorway, watching the dog and wondering what the *fuck* I'm supposed to do. Duke comes running back as soon as he's finished, happily slipping back into the house. I slam the door shut and turn the locks.

*I don't want to be here.*

But I don't want to call my parents, either. Our relationship is strained as it is. We go months without talking sometimes—and they only live an hour away. They were closer to Mason than me, and I'd hate to know what they'd think of this mess.

*Probably blame me for breaking up with him.*

I fill Duke's dog bowl and set it down on the tile floor for him before sifting through my phone to Emma's number. I hit call and take a seat on the couch. My eyes flicker to the fire poker by the fireplace, and I swallow hard.

*Guess I'll have to rely on that thing.*

"Wow, good morning," Emma groans groggily. "Why are you calling me at the ass-crack of dawn?"

"Things have...*escalated.*"

The sound of fumbling around fills the line. "What happened?" she asks, suddenly sounding wide awake. "Is it Mason?"

"Yeah," I answer her, glancing around the living room like he might be listening or something. "He took all the guns in my house...while I was sleeping."

Emma's quiet for a moment. "Whoa...I—did you call the police? Please tell me you called them."

"I did," I answer flatly. "And the deputy knows Mason. I don't think he took me seriously. I guess I'm going to change the locks, but I'm scared to leave and come back to him in the house." The words sound ridiculous coming out of my mouth. This is the kind of shit that only happens in the movies—or true crime documentaries. Maybe I've watched so many I unknowingly manifested it into reality.

*Yikes.*

"Come stay with me."

"I think Jared might murder me."

She pauses in a way that makes me uneasy. "Nah," she clears her throat. "But I don't blame you. He's more off than ever right now, but we can talk about that later."

"It sounds like we should talk about it—"

"No," she cuts me off. "He's just being a dick. Nothing new. You know how he is. Anyway, we need to talk about you. I think you need to get out of that house. If he seriously took all the guns out, I feel like that's a pretty big threat."

"Or he's toying with me because I shot at him yesterday."

"Uh, what? Why didn't you tell me?"

"I was still processing it," I tell her, and then go on to share the events that happened yesterday. She listens in silence.

"I would've shot his dick off."

"Good to know," I laugh, thankful for her sense of humor. "But I'm literally screwed. What if Mason tells the deputy that?"

"He was going to attack you, Lydia. You were just defending yourself, and you didn't even shoot him. It's his word against yours, but he *is* the one who took all your guns. He's disarmed you. That's a huge red flag to me. I don't think you should stay."

"I don't know where else to go. I don't want to put anyone else in danger—and you know how toxic my parents are." Honestly, I'm surprised Mason hasn't reached out to them yet, concocting some lunatic story about me losing my mind.

"You know..."

"What?"

Duke scratches at the door, and I go to it, sliding it open for him. He makes a beeline for the woods, and my heart sinks. I peer out into the overcast skies, but don't see anything. It's beginning to rain and could easily confuse someone into thinking it's nearly nighttime. Normally, I enjoy this kind of weather, but it's unsettling today.

*Please don't run off right now, Duke.*

"Did you hear me?" Emma's voice brings me back.

"Oh shit, no. I'm sorry." I run my fingers through my tangled blonde hair. I can't even bring myself to shower. I'm too concerned *Psycho* might play out in real life right there in my bathroom.

"Have you considered taking the job?"

My stomach knots up. "No. I already turned him down. I figure he left yesterday evening, anyway. It's probably too late."

*The offer will remain on the table if you change your mind.* His words echo in my mind. Did he actually mean it, though? And is that really the answer for this? I'm not one to back down from a fight. If I leave, it feels like I'm letting Mason win.

"I mean...I know. But we have a vacation house outside of Los Angeles...I could always tell Jared I want to take a trip? I'd be there—just in case. Or, you could offer to stay with me?"

"He wouldn't bend on the terms."

"Okay, so then just see what it entails, and if it goes wrong, I'm right there. His background check was clean, right? He's just super into your work. If I had someone like that when it comes to my writing, I'd be all over it."

"But you haven't met him," I reason. "I don't think it's the answer."

"Lydia, you are a sitting duck there in your cabin. Do something. Get out of there. Call someone to come stay with you. Please."

"I know," I groan, fighting the urge to cry again. "I just don't know what to do."

"Call the guy. You'll be thousands of miles from stupid Mason."

"Maybe I should call Mason."

"*No.* Stop this. I'm trying to help you come up with the fastest way to get away from your batshit crazy ex."

My eyes flicker to the shelf in the living room, scanning the pictures. And then my breath catches. "What. The. Hell." I jump to my feet, rushing to the empty picture frame.

"What is it?"

"He removed the picture of us from the frame in the living room."

Emma gasps. "Mason is being freaking *weird.* You have to get out of there."

"But I don't see how the answer is to run to the guy who *also* freaked me out."

"Okay, yeah, it sounds a little crazy...But like I said, I'll start packing. I could use the break from here. I doubt Jared will mind, anyway."

My heart pounds in my chest as I chew on my lip. Again, is this *really* the answer for me? Running off to take the deal I said I would never?

"I'll think about it," I finally say, just as Duke scratches on the door. I jump to my feet to open it, and in he steps, something stuck to his black collar. I bend down, thinking it's a leaf or branch.

My knees nearly give way.

It's a rose. A freaking rose. I slam the sliding glass door, locking it and dropping the bar. However, I can't help but peer out into the woods through the glass.

"Lydia?" Emma says into my ear.

I can barely breathe as I catch the outline of a figure standing in the tree line, tilting his head from behind a tree, a mask fashioned on his face. "I have to go," I say quickly, my voice shaking.

"Lydia—"

I hang up and immediately call 9-1-1, shaking as I put the phone up to my ear.

"9-1-1, what's your emergency?"

"Someone is outside of my house," I mutter into the phone. "Please hurry."

# Twelve

## Lydia

"You said he was here?" Deputy Briggins looks at me with an unamused expression, yet again.

I nod, my arms wrapped around my body. "He had on a strange mask with x's over the eyes."

"Right," he sighs, wearily looking around the woods.

"And he brought me a rose," I hold the flower out to him.

"Like, handed it to you?"

"He attached it to Duke's collar." My teeth chatter as I speak, cold rain battering my black raincoat. "I know it was Mason. Duke wouldn't accept a stranger."

He makes a face at me, peering down at my dog as he stands beside me. "He seems to have accepted me just fine."

My heart sinks. This guy isn't believing a freaking word that comes out of my mouth. "I—"

"Listen, with all due respect, I don't see anything here that's even disturbed. I see the rose, but maybe he's just trying to win you back over. Jim said he's taking the breakup pretty bad, but also mentioned you might...Maybe you need to talk to someone."

My mouth drops open, seeing right through the accusation. "I'm not unstable," I argue, shaking my head. *At least, I don't think so.*

"Why don't we call someone close to you? Jim said you've got some family that live north of here. Think they'd take you in for a few days?"

"I don't...I don't need my parents." The urge to cry is destroying my ability to argue, and honestly, I'm a little concerned that might end in him toting me off to a psych ward somewhere.

"Yeah..." his voice trails off as his eyes scan the ground.

Mine follow, and my heart stops as I catch sight of something glistening beneath the leaves. I reach down and pluck up the familiar pocketknife, holding it out to Deputy Briggins. "This is his knife."

Briggins narrows his eyes at it. "And you know that, because?"

"Because it's engraved." I point to the anniversary date on the side of the navy-blue exterior of the knife. "I bought it for him."

"And you don't think he could've dropped it at some point here before?"

My mouth hangs open stupidly. "I don't think so."

"But it's possible?" Deputy Briggins takes the knife from me.

My shoulders fall. "I guess."

"It's circumstantial at best, Ms. Waters."

I blink a couple of times, thanking the rain for hiding the tears streaking down my face right now. "I know I saw someone out here."

He meets my gaze, and I see it—the disbelief. "I don't know what to tell you. We don't have the resources to spend the whole damn day in the rain searching the woods for someone you thought you saw."

"But the knife? The rose?" I exasperate.

"Yeah...Maybe you should just call Mason and work it out. He's a good man. I've known him since he was a kid. He wouldn't do something like this. He wouldn't hurt a fly." The deputy slides the knife into his jacket pocket, and I realize this guy is leaving with the only proof I have it was Mason out here.

"So there's nothing you can do?" I ask him as I follow him back toward the front of the house.

"I'm working on the report for the stolen guns," he sighs, walking a little faster as the rain picks up. "I'll write this down, too, if that'll make you happy."

"Okay," I mumble, at a loss of what to even say.

"Again, I think you should get some rest and call someone," he glances over his shoulder at me. "You look like hell."

"Thanks for the information," I mutter under my breath as he heads to his car, and I head for the front door. *What a joke.* I watch as the car pulls out for the second time today.

He'll probably start spreading the rumors that I've lost my mind—and I don't know that he's wrong at this point, even with the rose, knife, and missing guns as evidence. It all points to a spurned lover losing his shit, but I'm losing mine, too, in the process.

And as I lock the door behind me, I realize Emma is right. I have to get out of here.

*Do I really want to do this?* The question floats around my mind as I pull out my phone, scrolling to Henry's contact. I check my watch, he's two hours behind me, but it's still within normal business hours. My heart beats unsteadily as I hit the call button.

I consider hanging up as it rings. And rings.

And rings.

I'm just about to really give in to failure when the call connects.

"Hello." His deep voice rattles my core, and I clench my thighs, embarrassed by the reaction. Since when does he get to me like this?

"Hi, um, this is Lydia."

He greets me with a chuckle. "I do have caller I.D., you know."

"Right..." my voice trails off. "I hope you had a nice flight."

"It was as good as it can be," he answers, the chuckle fading but the amusement remaining. "What can I do for you?"

"I was wondering..." I feel *so* stupid for the words coming out of my mouth. "You said the offer would remain on the table—did you mean that?"

"Yes."

"I think I'll accept it."

"Really?" His voice brightens to a point I start to wonder why I ever thought he was really that intimidating. He sounds...friendly. "That's great news. I can book your flight for tomorrow morning?"

I hesitate. "Is there...Is there any way you would be willing to book it for today?"

There're a few beats of silence. "I could probably arrange that. Let me see what I can do. And I take it the dog will need to be arranged for as well?"

"Yeah," I feel my face heat up. "That's asking for a lot. I'm sorry."

"No, I can figure it out. Give me about thirty minutes.

How long will it take you to be ready?"

"An hour tops."

"Perfect." He hangs up before I can even tell him goodbye. I take a deep breath and press my palm to my forehead, trying to breathe. Part of me is concerned I'm trading one evil for another—though maybe Mason was right.

Maybe I just automatically assume the worst in people.

Duke follows me around the house as I start packing. I force myself to take a quick shower, too, leaning the fire poker against the wall, but still in reach. It seems excessive, but I'm still convinced

Mason will show up at any point. I probably stoked the fire by calling the police...But isn't that what you're supposed to do? I know the drill. I know that they don't always take women seriously when stuff like this happens, but I really felt like I had a solid case.

My phone buzzes as I step out of the shower, and I swoop it up, seeing a message from Henry.

> Your flight is scheduled for 4PM at Will Rogers Airport. Call (469) 555-2356. I'll have a car to pick you up when you arrive.

His text is confusing, but I press the number he's listed and give it a call.

"This is Devon with Angelic Private Jet Charters. How can I help you?"

I gape at the realization of flying privately. "This is Lydia Waters. I was told I have a flight at 4 o'clock today."

"Ah yes," he chuckles. "Let me get you the information on that."

\*\*\*

A few hours later, Duke and I are boarding a private jet— and it's surreal. I don't know how I feel about it, honestly. Though, Emma, on the other hand, is more than hyped for me. She's already swearing she'll be joining me, but I still feel unnerved about the entire thing. I didn't have any more strange happenings while I got ready to leave, and I locked my house up tight, though I'm not sure what good that did. If Mason wants in, he'll get in.

"Can I get you something to drink?" The flight attendant smiles as Duke sits panting in the seat across from me.

I shake my head, feeling nauseous. "No, thank you."

She nods. "I can get you something to help if you're not feeling well."

I stare up at her pretty dark hair, pulled back into a tight bun. She's probably younger than me, and has beautiful, deep brown eyes. "I should be fine."

"Okay, well, let me know if you need anything."

I give her the best smile I can muster, turning to gaze out the window. I take in the thick cover of clouds and wonder what exactly I'm flying into. I haven't signed the contract. I could back out once I get there.

But then what?

I shudder at the thought of going back to my house. As much as I love my little cabin in the woods, leaving it is a freaking relief. This is the safest I've felt since breaking things off with Mason. And all the creeping he's been doing has annihilated any ounce of heartache I might've felt. My feelings are dead and gone.

But maybe they were all along.

I lean my head against the window and shut my eyes, drifting off to a dream that greets me with a pair of icy grayish blue eyes—and that's fine by me.

# Thirteen

## Henry

"Can we talk about this?" Jude asks me the moment I step through the door of my beachside house. It's not in Los Angeles, exactly. It's further north, but I can't let the exact location be disclosed, so I keep it under a false address *in* Los Angeles. It's the smaller of my houses at only three-thousand square feet, but the luxury is unmatched.

"Talk about what?" I head straight past him, heading for my bedroom.

"Talk about the fact that you're bringing a woman here under completely false pretenses." He follows me, his footsteps heavy against the bamboo flooring. Jude is just as tall as me, but he's a little leaner—and definitely not a fighter. He belongs behind the computer.

"It's not a false pretense," I counter, swinging open the black bulletproof door. "She's going to write a book—just like we discussed."

"But this whole thing isn't about a book." He adjusts the dark-rimmed glasses on his face. They stand out on his light complexion, paired with blondish red hair. "You're bringing her here to never let her leave."

"Meh, details."

"This could be a mess. She could claim you've kidnapped her."

"Oh stop, for fuck's sake," I snap at him as I toss my bag onto the black comforter. "I swear, you're such a downer. I don't have time for this shit. You have a house, you don't have to be here."

He sighs. "This is where we *work*."

"You can work from home then."

He lets out a frustrated breath. "I don't like it."

"You've made that clear already. We don't have to beat a dead horse." I ignore the annoyed look on his face, unpacking as quickly as possible. She needs to believe I've been back since yesterday. The mask and the placement of the knife I found in Mason's truck seems to have done the trick.

And now the real fun begins.

I shove a pair of jeans into my black dresser. "Will you go pick her up?"

His eyes widen. "No."

My shoulders slump with this. "Don't be so hardheaded. Just go pick her up and be nice."

His lip curls up. "Why can't you go pick her up?"

"It'll be better if you do. I know she's leery of me."

"Hard to imagine why," he replies flatly.

I ignore the jab. "You've got a friendly aura about you, and I need her to feel like she has a friend here—other than me."

"Her friend has a vacation house fifteen minutes away, and she booked a flight. I looked into it when you had me digging into her phone records. Are you sure she's not just using you for a flight? There's no contract signed yet."

I consider the idea but shake my head. "No, I don't think so. She has the funds to pay for her own flight. I don't think she'd need me to do it."

"Touche," Jude shrugs. "I just have a bad feeling about it."

"You always have a bad feeling about everything," I scoff, pulling my gun from its locked safety box beneath my bed. He watches me carefully. "I've got to put some eyes on our next target."

"So what? I'm supposed to bring her back here alone?"

"I'll be back before then...*hopefully*. If I'm not back in time, just have her stay in the spare room next to mine. Help her get settled in. Make her some fucking tea or something. She's been through hell."

He narrows his eyes. "I can imagine. Why don't you—"

"Don't ask questions right now. It's better for you to go into it honestly. Her flight will be here at six. They got a late start because of the storms."

"Was it the storms?"

I shoot him a wink. "Who knows." I pat him on the back and head for the door. Jude is my best friend, and while I'm as jealous as a psycho can be over Lydia...

I know he won't cross any lines. Not in that way.

I just have to hope his humanity doesn't overpower his loyalty. It's another reason I take care of the groundwork. He's better with all the coverup.

"Also," Jude says from behind me, "I created a digital trail for Mason. The cleanup crew took his phone to Vermont. He's got some old college friends in that area, and they took it to a bar. Created a video of him going into a bar and leaving. You know the drill."

I nod as I descend the steps and open the garage door. "I knew there's a reason I keep you around."

"Here's the address for tonight." Jude pulls out his phone and sends it to my phone. "The guy has a wife and kids."

I frown. "How old are the kids?"

"Teenagers," Jude rattles off. "They're not around much. From what I gather, home life isn't so great. The oldest daughter is nineteen, in college, and living away. The youngest girl is seventeen. She spends a lot of time at her boyfriend's house."

"And the wife?"

"No idea. She's never out and about. No socials. She stays home all the time. There're rumors floating around that he won't let her leave."

"Wonder if she ordered this," I muse. I love it when the wives of abusers have the funds to take them out. It makes my job all the more enjoyable.

"No idea. Good luck though."

I give his shoulder a squeeze and head for my black Mercedes SUV. It's not really my type, but it's the best way *not* to stand out. I have other cars for that. "Don't be late picking Lydia up," I warn him, before closing the car door.

The fucker rolls his eyes at me.

I put the car in reverse, laughing to myself. I know he'll pick her up and do as I say, even if he gripes about it. We're a good team, and I might have gone off the deep end with my obsession with Lydia, but it's only going to get worse from here.

Anticipation strains against my jeans. It won't be long, and I'll be making her mine. I know that. There's tension between us, and she's going to give in. However, how soon depends on how I play the game. I need her to trust me. It's going to take that to handle the truth when it comes to the surface.

The drive to Beverly Hills is long and grueling, the traffic annoying. I don't like living close to the larger cities, but most of my hits don't live out in the boonies. High-class sickos need to flash their lives in front of as many people as possible. I pull up against the curb, parking across from the stucco modern mansion. It's charming to some degree, though maybe a little overdone.

I settle in my seat, focusing my gaze on the house. There're so many cameras around these days that we have to switch out license plates and vehicles constantly, but it's a low cost to pay to keep from going to jail.

Though I *do* have connections everywhere.

My eyes focus on the front door, but my mind drifts back to Lydia. I've done so well focusing on the goal of getting her to accept my offer, but now? Now all I can think about is those glassy emerald eyes, taunting the evil in me. I want to rip her to shreds.

And I hope like hell I didn't underestimate her.

I won't know until I can get closer to her, learn her soul and what makes her pretty mind tick with so many dark images. My mind pictures her beneath me, but that fades as the front door opens of the Carlson residence.

Out steps my target.

*Bart Carlson.*

"What a name," I mumble as I watch him, dawning a tuxedo as he heads toward the Lamborghini in the driveway. I peer at the ajar front door, expecting someone else to join him. However, when a blonde woman clad in a pair of flannel pajamas pulls the door, I see exactly why people think what they do.

She looks *rough.*

And even from the distance I'm sitting at now, I can see the light bruising on her cheek. I shake my head. Who knows what else this guy is into.

He looks back at her, gesturing something that's too easy to interpret.

*Go back inside.*

Carlson looks around, a concerned expression on his face.

*Yeah, I saw it, dipshit.*

And if I wasn't so excited for my guest to arrive, I would take care of him right now. But I'll have to wait until he's not going anywhere. It's better if they're not missed for a while. That always complicates things.

But tonight is perfect to get a layout of the house.

# Fourteen

## Lydia

I watch the blond headed, somewhat nerdy looking man loading up my bags into the back of a white Lexus SUV. "So..."

He looks up at me with a raised brow. "What?"

"Where do you want me to sit? And him, too?" I gesture down to Duke, who's still panting from three and a half hours of trauma. He's never been on a plane before, and he was ready to get off the moment we landed.

"Uh, the car preferably," he says, making a face. He closes the back hatch and sighs. "Will he sit in the backseat?"

I nod as the man opens the back door. "Are you an Uber driver?" The question sounds so freaking stupid, but I feel lost. I just took a flight on a private jet, and now some guy I've never seen before in my life is picking me up and driving me somewhere.

I need to know if I'm covered.

"I am *not* an Uber driver," the guy laughs as I load Duke into the backseat, using the clip on his harness to buckle him in. "Not a Lyft driver, either."

"Oh," I say blankly as I let him shut the door. I fold my arms across my chest as I back away. I mean, now that Duke is in the car, I'm going, too, but still. I feel uneasy.

"I'm Jude." He gives me a lopsided smile, sticking out his hand.

I study his face, his hazel eyes much warmer than Henry's icy gaze. His nose is stubby, but he's not unattractive. I shake his hand. I've already gone this far, might as well accept it.

"He's my partner," Jude tells me as he opens the passenger door for me. "I'll be at the house a lot." I don't know if he meant that as some sort of reassurance, but it works. I relax a little as he closes the door and walks around to the driver's side. He climbs in and grabs the seatbelt.

"What do you do for work?" The question comes out awkward, but I haven't been able to find anything on Henry Bayne when it comes to his current career—and clearly, he's wealthy.

"Tech contractors," Jude answers curtly, putting the car in drive. I don't know exactly what that means, but I don't press. There's a lot of things I don't know, and right now, I'm just happy to be a long freaking way from Mason.

I lean back against the seat. Despite having a nap on the flight, I *still* feel exhausted. I didn't realize how unnerved I was about it all until I got far enough away to feel safe. Somewhat, anyway.

"He may or may not be there when we arrive." Jude's voice is flat and unemotional, but not unfriendly. "Are you hungry or anything?"

I shake my head. "No, I'm good. Thank you, though."

He eyes me, studying my face a beat or two longer than I prefer. "So, what's the book about?"

"Um," I hesitate. "I don't know yet. I wasn't planning on taking the job. It was kind of a last-minute thing. From what I gather, he's wanting a crime thriller mixed with some romance."

Jude cracks a smile. "Sounds about right."

I breathe out a sigh. "So how far is it to his house?"

"About an hour or so—maybe more," Jude answers, not reacting to the way my eyes widen. "It's outside of town on the coast. He likes his privacy—I think we all do."

I nod, trying not to internally freak out. "My friend has a vacation house out here."

"Yeah?" He turns to me. "You ever been to it?"

"No," I answer him, gripping my bag on my lap. "I don't get out much."

"Well, you'll probably like the house then," Jude chuckles, giving me a half-hearted smile. "It's got a great view if you like the ocean."

"Yeah, I've never seen the Pacific Ocean." He nods. "Well, you'll get to shortly."

And that's the end of the conversation. I spend the rest of the ride in silence, staring out the window as we drive further from the city and further down the coast. The houses grow further apart, though still closer than what I'm used to.

Jude eventually turns off the main highway to a more residential road, taking it another few miles. Finally, a modern, luxurious beach house comes into view. My lips part as I take in the white and black colors. It's elegant—and mysterious.

"Home sweet home," Jude mutters, hitting the garage door opener. It's got a four-car garage, which seems like a little much, but as we pull in, there're only two cars. A black Ferrari and gray Bronco. "He's not here."

I turn to Jude, seeing the frustration in his expression. I don't know what to say to him, so I push the passenger door open, sliding out and heading for the backseat to get Duke.

Jude climbs out and heads to grab my luggage—which isn't much. I was so ready to get out of my house I just threw everything in there...

And now I'm hoping I didn't forget anything.

"Come on," Jude jerks his head as he stands with the garage door open. He hits the button and the overhead door jars, sliding toward the ground.

I nod, figuring I'll take Duke out in a little while. I fish my phone out of my pocket as I follow Jude. I drop a pin and send it to Emma.

> This is where I'm staying if something happens.

My phone instantly pings with a response.

> That's only fifteen minutes from my place. It's a good area. Enjoy it!

I like the message, so I don't trip up the steep stairs. The scent of sandalwood and Henry's cologne hits my lungs as Jude opens the door into the warm lit mudroom area. It's the kind of house you see in the magazines, perfectly put together and appearing like no one lives there at all.

"I'll show you to your room," Jude says as he kicks on the light in an ornate kitchen, following the same black and white scheme as the rest of the house. There's minimal décor, and what is hung on the walls is abstract.

And it only adds to the mystery.

However, I'm met with a wall of windows overlooking the crashing waves and desolate beach. It's *breathtaking*.

"It's got a good view."

"Yeah, most definitely," I say, looking over to Jude, who's watching me with careful eyes. I feel like a science experiment or something.

"Let's keep going. I'm ready to set these down."

I nod, though my eyes keep going back to the ocean. Duke stops to try and smell everything, but I tug him onward, keeping up with Jude. We head through a living room with black leather furniture and white carpet, which draws my attention away from the gorgeous waterfront sight.

*Oh boy.*

I glance down at Duke. I'll have to keep an eye on him. Dogs and white carpet don't always go together...Especially when it's *my* dog.

"Your room is the first door on the left," Jude gestures to a black door as we enter a long hallway. "Henry's room is that one." He points to the one at the end of the hallway. "You have a bathroom attached to your room, so you don't have to leave for any reason."

"Except to eat," I point out.

He laughs easily. "Yeah, that's true. I have no doubt Henry will feed you well. He won't let you starve or fend for yourself."

I nod, not sure if I'm relieved or not.

"Upstairs is another spare room and office. You probably won't have a reason to go up there, but that's what it is. That's where I stay if I need to crash here."

"Do you do that often?"

He looks me dead in the eye, his voice flat. "No, but I have a feeling I will be more often."

I'm not sure how to take that so I choose to just smile. I know he didn't mean it in a romantic way based on his tone, and I lean more toward the idea of a babysitter.

But surely, he's not talking about me.

I step into my new room behind him, taking in the large queen-sized bed. It's basic, but nice. The comforter is black, which is easily becoming a common theme in the house. There's a wooden dresser and nightstand on either side. A small writing desk sits in the corner with a leather desk chair.

"This is the bathroom." Jude nods to the open double doors.

I peer in, seeing the large jacuzzi tub and walk in stone shower. "It's nice."

"Glad you're happy with it."

I nod. "I need to take my dog out...Is that okay?"

Jude laughs. "You're not a prisoner or something. You can go out through the kitchen door. It's the straightest shot to the beach if that's where you'd like to go."

"Thanks," I swallow hard and lead Duke back through the house. As pristine as it all is, it's strikingly comfortable. There's nothing threatening about the house—or Jude for that matter.

And maybe once I get to know him a little bit, I won't find anything unnerving about Henry, either.

"Oh wait," Jude calls out to me as I reach for the handle.

I stop, turning to look at him as he walks toward me, something in his hand. I furrow my brow as he holds out a key.

"It's the key for the house. There's a keypad, but um." He hesitates, letting out a breath. "It's just not reliable. Use the key if you get locked out, go on a walk, or whatever."

I nod slowly, taking the key from him. I shove it into the pocket of my faded jeans and open the door the rest of the way. Duke and I slip out into the evening, the sun having already set. However, the warm, salty air feels like the hug I've desperately needed as I make my way across the back deck.

"Maybe this was a good idea," I tell Duke as my feet hit the sandy ground. We make our way closer to the dark waves gently meeting the sandy beach. I slide out of my Vans and pull my socks off, setting them to the side.

We approach the edge of the water. It's not the first time Duke has seen the ocean, but he takes a few moments before allowing the waves to wash over his paws. I wade into the warm waters immediately, not even caring as it soaks my jeans to the middle of my calves. I kick the water up, and Duke jumps playfully, his eyes lighting up.

A giggle escapes from my throat as we play, and for the first time in a couple of days, I forget about everything.

And it feels so freaking good.

# Fifteen

## Henry

Her laughs cut through the air like a knife, penetrating my chest all the way to my heart. And for a moment, I feel a little less dead inside. Every ounce of me wants to go out there and join her, but if I did...

I wouldn't know what the fuck I was doing.

I don't let loose, and unless it's dry, twisted humor, I don't laugh. But I like it when she does.

"What'd you think of Carlson?" Jude asks, adjusting himself in the seat at the island bar. His body is angled away from where Lydia and Duke are, and I prefer it that way.

"I think he's at a minimum a wife beater. I got a solid layout of the house. Seems like the teenagers' rooms are located in the west wing. The master is in the east." I recall slipping through the front door, which wasn't armed with a security system. "The wife is a pill popper. She was passed out cold when I entered."

Jude frowns. "That's sad."

"I guess you have to deal with it some way, and based on the information you pulled on her, she doesn't have anywhere to go if she were to leave him."

"You could just add her to the guest list here."

I don't laugh at the joke. "Lydia isn't a guest. This is her home now."

"Yeah, you're messed up."

Ignoring him, I continue with our assignment. "I placed cameras throughout the house—including his locked office. You should be able to pick up what's going on, and then we can decide when to take him out."

Jude nods. "I'll start surveillance. If you need me, I'll be upstairs." He slides off the bar stool and rolls his shoulders. "Also, you might want to be gentle with her." He gestures through the glass to Lydia as she prances around in the waves with her dog. "She's leery. I wouldn't be surprised if she has an escape route planned."

My jaw ticks with irritation. "Lydia will be signing the contract tonight, and if she tries to run, certain measures will be taken."

Jude's face remains emotionless. "She has no idea she's stepped into hell."

*I can make it heaven for her.*

My gaze returns to the glass, peering out as Lydia and Duke start making their way toward the house. I have motorized blinds that cover the wall of windows, but I left them open for her arrival. I don't want her to think this place is as unwelcoming as it really is.

As Lydia and Duke make it up the steps, I take in the sight of her soaked body, her jeans clinging to her hips, the fabric darkened from the upper thigh down. My mouth waters at the idea of peeling them from her body and drying her off myself.

Lydia opens the door and sticks her head in, her eyes growing wide as they meet mine. Her hair is a beautiful mess, damp from the ocean spray and falling out of the bun on her head. "Um..."

"Good evening." The words come out smoother than I feel on the inside. Internally, I want to devour her.

"Do you have a towel I could use? Duke is a little...wet."

"And so are you."

She blushes, her high cheek bones painted with a delicate hue of crimson. "Yeah, but I don't want him to ruin your carpet..."

I smile at her, noticing the small tremble in her shoulders. "It's just carpet. It can be replaced, but I'll be right back." I push off from where I'm leaning and make my way to the hallway linen closet, the monster tapping on my brain.

*I could make her undress outside. Refuse to give her the towel. Bend her over the rails...*

"Nope," I mutter, grabbing a couple of gray towels and shoving them under my arm. I don't give it or my dick another thought as I make my way back to the kitchen, and hand the towels to her. "There's a woman who comes once a week to clean, cook, and do laundry, so you can put them in the hamper when you're done."

She purses her lips at me, and I can tell she wants to ask questions. However, Lydia remains quiet as she releases the door and steps outside. I take a breath, sharply exhale, and then join her on the back deck.

"I'll dry your dog off," I offer, reaching for one of the towels.

"Oh, you don't have to—"

"I know I don't," I cut in, pulling the fabric from her arms and going for Duke. He recognizes me and begins to wag his tail in a greeting.

Lydia remains frozen, staring at us. "He doesn't usually like strangers."

*Good thing I'm not one.*

I shrug, rubbing his soaked fur down with the towel. Thankfully, he doesn't shed all that much, but even if he did...I'd deal with it.

Anything for Lydia. I watch her from the corner of my eye as she rolls the towel down her body, stopping at the wet jeans.

"Just take them off."

"Excuse me?" Her voice jumps an octave.

"The jeans?" I chuckle, running the towel under Duke's body and looking up at her.

"I'm not undressing—"

"I won't watch," I lie, looking away from her. Maybe I'm not so great at keeping the reins tight internally.

She's quiet for a few moments, but then lets out a sharp sigh. "I'll just change in my room."

*Yeah, that won't be your room for long.*

"Suit yourself," I say flatly, though disappointment rattles my body. I finish drying off Duke and straighten myself up. The smell of wet dog permeates the air, but I bite back the complaint.

She wraps the towel around her shoulders, eyeing me as I reach for the door, opening it for the two of them. "Thank you," she mumbles under her breath as they step through the opening.

"You can have the rest of tonight to settle in." I shut and lock the door.

Lydia looks up at me, clinging to her towel and the leash of her dog with one hand. "Okay. Tomorrow we can go over the general synopsis of the book?" Her voice takes an air of professionalism.

And it's adorable, considering she's standing in my kitchen drenched.

"First, you have to sign this." I retrieve the contract from the counter.

"Oh yeah," she mumbles. Lydia walks over and I hand her a pen for her free hand. I flip to the signature page and she scribbles her name across the line.

*Finally.*

"Thanks, I have a list for you of what I'd like included in the book. I'll give it to you in the morning."

She nods, and I swear the mention of work seems to relax her as her grip loosens on the towel and she sets the pen down. "That sounds good." Her eyes flicker around the room, the only light on being the warm chandelier above the island. "Your house is beautiful."

"Hmm."

"I bet you get that a lot," she laughs, the tone nervous and uneasy.

"Not really." *Because no one ever comes here.*

"Okay, well," she pushes a few strands of damp hair from her eyes. "I guess I will see you in the morning."

"If you need anything, I'm the door at the end of the hallway. Jude is upstairs tonight. He's working late."

She bobs her head and then tugs at Duke, the two of them scurrying off to her room. I watch her as she goes, her wet jeans clinging to her ass. And the moment the door closes behind her, I run my hands over my face.

*How the hell am I supposed to do this?*

I make my way to my room, hitting the switch to shut the blinds and turn off the light in the kitchen. Darkness slowly encases the house, and it allows me to breathe a little easier. I don't belong in the warm glow of a kitchen light with a woman like Lydia, but here I am, forcing her to do it.

Well, not in totality, I guess.

She *is* here on her own accord even if it took some manipulation—and that's about the only thing I have going for me. Because as I shut the door behind me, I fucking lose it. Desire and lust burn through my veins, and I no longer fight it. I shed my clothes from my body, step into the bathroom, and start the black-tiled shower.

My cock throbs in my hand as I stand under the stream of water, scalding my shoulders. I squeeze my eyes shut, and let my mind run wild, mentally placing Lydia right here in this shower.

*I pin her bare body against the wall, my cock pressed into her lower stomach and my fingers tracing the water droplets on her throat. "Are you going to be a good girl for me?"*

*She whimpers in response, her emerald eyes widening as my grip tightens, the end of my fingertips pressing into her delicate, creamy skin. Her body shivers against me.*

*"Say it," I demand from her, forcing her chin upward with a flick of my wrist.*

*Her hands fly to my chest, pressing against my skin as if she might push me away—but she doesn't. Instead, she holds my gaze. "I'll be a good girl...for you."*

*I bite down on my lip and squeeze, taking her breath away for only a few seconds before releasing. She gasps for air but is cut off by my mouth, refusing to let her take what she needs. My tongue runs along her bottom lip before encasing her entirely, possessively claiming her as my own.*

*A moan slips from her throat as she kisses me back, tickling my hand. I squeeze in response, but not hard enough to stifle the sensation.*

*I want more.*

*I want that pussy wrapped around my cock, taking every inch of me. My lips break from hers, and I flip her around. Lydia lets out a cry as I roughly pin her against the wall, dipping my hips and pushing inside of her.*

*"Oh fuck," she cries out as I slip my hand through her hair, tugging her head back to look at me.*

*"You're mine," I growl, thrusting the rest of the way into her. My hips slam into her ass, and her eyes grow glassy as moans fill the shower.*

But it's just in my head.

And as cum fills my hand, my release short and unsatisfactory, I let out a frustrated groan. Now that the woman is in my house, and the high of stalking her is gone, I'm a ticking time bomb.

And it's only a matter of time before I explode.

# Sixteen

## Lydia

Duke whines at the door of my room, and I sigh, picking up my phone from the nightstand. I wearily look at the time, and see that I've missed a message from Emma. It's only five o'clock in the morning—but that's seven back at home.

> How is it? Sorry I've been busy.

> It's fine... And I think it's good?

I exit out of the message thread and gaze around the room as Duke's voice grows in volume. I reach for my black fuzzy robe, and climb out of bed. I'd rather risk going out looking like a mess than risk Duke waking anyone up.

"Let's go," I grab the leash and harness and fit it to my oversized hound, blinking away the sleep from my eyes. I reach for the door and open it, peeking out and looking both ways. It's dead silent.

And pitch black.

My heart beats uneasily in my chest as I retreat, grabbing my phone. I turn on the flashlight function, and make my way down the hallway, holding my breath. Clearly, no one is awake and the last thing I want to do is disturb them.

Duke's paws patter against the flooring—which I assume is some sort of bamboo laminate? I don't know. My knowledge of luxurious, high-end living is minimal. I'm tempted to turn on the kitchen light as we enter, but I don't see the switch. And even if I did, I'm not sure I could bring myself to do it. I feel like an intruder at the moment, though I did get the best sleep I've gotten in a few days.

My eyes shift to slits as I try to make out the lock on the door.

"If you open that, an alarm is gonna go off," a deep voice startles me, sending me sideways.

Where the hell did *he* come from?

Henry chuckles as he passes me, moving so quiet he could be a ghost. He reaches up to a keypad beside the door and types in a code, a chime following as the system disarms.

"Thanks," I choke out, as he turns to face me. It's only then I realize he's missing a shirt, and I can't stop myself as my eyes pour over his muscular, fit chest and abdomen...covered in ink I can't make out in the dark. However, all the tattoos stop before they reach his neckline or past where a short-sleeve T-shirt would end.

"Work prevents me from having any visible tattoos," he answers the question in my head.

"Right." I rip my eyes from him, fumbling with the lock on the door. My breath catches as his presence grows nearer, his looming figure casting a sudden warmth against my skin. His fingers slide past mine, and with a *click,* the door unlocks. My head grows light as he pulls the door inward, the cool morning breeze kissing my skin.

"It can be a little tricky," he hums in a low voice.

The moonlight casts a glow across his face, and my heart stutters as his eyes are riddled with trouble, appearing dark and stormy, rather than icy.

And I've never been so mesmerized by the change.

Duke tugs the leash right out of my hand, taking off across the deck and ripping me out of the trance.

"Shit," I cry out, spinning around to chase him.

"I'll put up a fence," Henry laughs from behind me as I chase after him, catching his leash just before he makes it to the stairs. "Nice reflexes."

My face burns as I slow down, wishing I could melt into the sand around me. I'm not sure that I even heard Henry correctly when he said something about a fence, and I can feel his eyes boring into the back of me as I let Duke do his business.

*I should've gotten dressed before coming out here.*

*Or at least brushed my teeth.*

I inwardly cringe and make the promise to myself that I'll take care of that as soon as I get back inside—and then never do it again. In order to keep from looking behind me, I cast my gaze across the beach, drinking in the view of the ocean waves. It's calm and peaceful, working to lessen the way my mind is racing.

But then my phone vibrates in the pocket of my robe. I forgot I even put it there. I dig it out and throw a glance back where Henry was. He's disappeared. It's unnerving how he moves around without even a little noise.

But not nearly as unnerving as *Mom* lighting up my phone screen.

"Hello?" I answer, only because she never calls.

"So you and Mason broke up?"

*Uh oh.*

I facepalm myself. "Yeah...I was meaning to tell you, but—"

"He's run off to Vermont," she snaps, her tone accusatory and sharp. "Did you know that? The poor guy is heartbroken, and he told Jim that you were the one who called it off. And then you called the cops on him?"

I shake my head, trying to process what she's saying. It's relieving to know he's on the other side of the country—but I still have to defend myself when it comes to my mother. "He stole my guns out of the house—"

"He said he felt like you were unstable."

"Well, I'm not," I say with confidence I don't feel. "And I don't want to talk about all of this if you're just going to take his side. He completely creeped me out, sneaking around in the woods by my house and trying to scare me. He's a psycho."

She lets out a sharp breath, and I brace. "I don't know."

My shoulders relax. She's taking this much better than I thought. "Well, it is what it is. Things haven't been good between us for years."

"I know. He just couldn't figure out what he wanted in life."

*That's one way to put it.*

"Do you want us to help you pack his things?"

I shake my head—like she can see it. "Uh, no. I'm not home, and he doesn't have anything there. He took it all the last time we got into a fight."

"Toxic," she mutters, which also serves to surprise me. I always thought they were on Mason's side when it came to our relationship, but maybe I was wrong. "Where are you?"

"California," I answer. "I took a job for a client and was required to come out here for the duration of the job." I make it sound like it's normal, even though everything about what I'm feeling is *not* normal.

"Like a vacation, I guess."

I don't argue with her, letting the silence fill the line as I glance back to the house. The curtains that covered the windows are now pulled away, and there, I can see the outline of someone. I shiver at the thought of his eyes transfixed on me.

"Karen is convinced Mason is missing."

I wrinkle my nose in confusion, my stomach knotting up but my voice emotionless. "I thought you said he was in Vermont."

"That's where he was last seen yesterday, but he hasn't talked to anyone since. I think they're going to report it."

"He's probably just passed out drunk somewhere," I scoff, heading back toward the beach house. "I'm sure he'll show up. It wouldn't be the first time he's done something like this."

"Well, you're a little cold."

"He burned me, and I'm done with it," I clarify. "I'll talk to you later. I need to get to work."

We hang up without the use of *I love you*, because that's not a phrase that's ever been used in that household. I'm not even sure my parents say it to each other. I shove my phone back into my pocket and trudge back to the house, trying to push the thought of Mason out of my mind. He'd run off to Vermont before, making the ungodly long drive straight through just so he could make it in time to hit the bars with one of his old friends.

As I step inside, I'm met with the scent of fresh coffee, and I look over to see Henry, now fully dressed in dark jeans and a white T-shirt. His wavy dark hair is fixed in a way that's unkempt yet sophisticated. My mind flashes with the image of my fingers threaded through it.

*Whoa. That's a bad idea.*

Men are nothing but bad news, and I'm pretty sure Henry is the epitome of it. He's too handsome and mysterious to not be.

"You don't have to keep him on a leash." His voice draws my gaze back to his eyes.

*Was I staring? Jeez, I hope not.*

"Are you sure?" I ask the question stupidly, and Henry nods in response, filling a mug with coffee. I lean over Duke, removing his harness and leash. He takes off across the kitchen...

Right for Henry.

"You can hang it there," Henry gestures to a hook beside the door as he pats Duke's head. I turn to the small, black u- shaped hook. I don't know if it was there before. It probably was.

I swallow hard as I do as I'm told, feeling his eyes on me. I *really* should've taken a moment to at least look in the mirror before I walked out of the room.

"Here." Henry extends the mug. "Let me know if it needs any-thing."

Slowly, I walk close enough to him to take it from his hands. "Thanks."

*Ugh, I tell him that a lot.*

"Yeah, no problem."

"I'm sorry if I woke you up this morning," I tell him, taking a sip of the warm liquid. It's got just enough creamer to sweeten it, but not enough to take away the bite of the coffee itself.

"Don't apologize to me." Henry's jaw ticks beneath a light shad-ow of facial hair. It's just enough to draw out my urge to run my fingers across it, distracting me from the strange demand.

"Sorr—"

He stops me with a look. "Your existence is not an apology, Lydia. Stop it."

"Okay," I nearly whisper. I rock to my heels, feeling a tension fill the room that wasn't there before. I'm reminded once again as to why I chose not to take the job. Henry has warm, friendly moments. And then moments like this—that I don't understand.

"Here's the list I promised you." He slides a folded-up piece of paper across the white granite countertop. "I came up with it on the go."

I nod, taking it from him. "I'll take a look at it and then get started on a general plot. I'll go over that with you, and then we'll go from there?"

His lip curls upward. "We'll rendezvous around nightfall. I have some work to get done until then."

I swallow the knot in my throat. The husky words roll through my body like a flame to gasoline, and my heart struggles to keep up with the sensation, beating wildly in my chest. Does he *know* he's this alluring?

He gives me a light smile as he heads for the garage, whipping open the door and disappearing down the steps. I stand there like an idiot, blinking my eyes until I hear the start of an engine. No matter how terrifying he might be, my attraction is strengthening.

And I'm either falling into temptation or recklessness.

...Or both.

But either way, I need to get him out of my head.

# Seventeen

## Henry

"He's a basket case," I tell Jude the moment I step into the cave upstairs. It's lined with monitors, hard drives, filing cabinets—the whole fucking works. No one comes up here except for my partner. It's like the room in the castle where the beast keeps the wilting rose. Only I don't have a dying flower, just a bunch of evidence of deceased people.

Probably equally as frightening.

But there aren't any physical bodies here, so that counts for something.

"I'm aware."

"He travels around town without actually stopping anywhere," I huff, plopping down in the chair. "It was literally three hours of playing car chase—only he had no idea I was chasing him."

Jude scrolls through something on his dual screen monitor. "Yeah, but he hasn't seen anyone for mental health problems. He act paranoid?" His hazel eyes pull from the screen to me.

I shake my head. "More like erratic."

"I didn't catch any drug use on the cameras," Jude says with a sigh. "And as far as I can tell, I don't think the guy has any kind of social media presence."

"Which is odd, given his lifestyle."

"Agreed," Jude mutters, going back to typing. "He's not linked to any organized crime groups either."

"Maybe someone just doesn't like him."

"And that someone is his wife?" My partner leans back in his chair. "Seems like that's all we can come up with—and it doesn't really matter who called him in. That's not really our problem."

I nod, but my stomach flips. "Something feels off about it."

"Since when do you have a conscience when it comes to hits?" Jude raises a brow at me. "Even Cher doesn't pull that kind of humanity out of you."

"I'm not soft." *Maybe distracted, though.* When I came in from trailing him, I almost went straight to Lydia's room instead of coming up to talk with Jude. She's just too damn tempting. I start to sweat at the thought of getting her alone. Taking a deep breath, I try to focus on Jude, pushing the thoughts away.

"Speaking of, have you talked to Cher?"

"No. It's better that we don't speak often."

"Right, but you'll bait a poor stranger into living with you to satisfy some sick need."

"You know," I snap, pushing myself up out of the black leather desk chair. "You screwed up the file on her in the first place, and I haven't held that over your head once."

Jude runs his fingers through his sandy hair. "Yeah, and I'm sorry about that—but then again, I'm really not. You're screwing her life up."

"We snuff out lives for a living," I growl at him, frustration rolling through my body. "I don't give a shit what you think about it, Jude."

He lets out a sharp sigh but doesn't say anything. His eyes drift back to the screen as he switches back to the camera monitors.

And what happens draws *both* of our eyes.

"What the..."

In walks Carlson through the grand entryway of his mansion, and it's clear he's fucked up. His wife greets him, but he ignores her, slipping off from the camera's view and climbing the stairs to the second floor.

"Follow him."

"I am," Jude snaps, bringing the shot into full screen.

Carlson stumbles down the hallway and stops outside of his office. He reaches for the doorknob and stops again, glancing around. He then unlocks it and pushes it open.

"Suspicious dipshit." Jude swaps to the office camera I put in the house. "Did you see anything weird when you went in there?"

I shake my head. "There was nothing that stood out. I didn't go digging deep. The desk drawers were locked and I didn't feel like picking them. I didn't know when he'd be home...And you know, we're not hired to learn anything about them. Just to knock them."

Jude nods, because he gets it. However, out of the two of us, he tends to take more of an interest in their everyday lives. In the end, it can be helpful, but I don't think it adds all that much to the job—other than excitement for him. He gets off on knowing them and then rearranging their digital trail.

My eyes stay focused on the screen as Carlson unlocks the bottom drawer of his desk, pulling out a cigar box. "Hopefully, that's just more..." I stare at what I thought would be drugs—or sexual material.

Nope. It's a piece of paper. Talk about anticlimactic. But still, curiosity is a bitch.

"Zoom in," I lean over Jude's shoulder, forgetting all about the tiff we had moments ago.

"Looks like a will." Jude's eyes are in slits as he rolls the mouse, getting as close as he can. But the footage is too grainy to make out much more than the header.

"So maybe someone wants him dead over money," I suggest, rolling away from the computer. "That's not anything new."

Jude opens his mouth to say something, but a knock on the door causes us both to freeze. I roll my shoulders and trot to the door, my heart pounding at the thought of her seeking me out—or seeing what's in this room. Talk about having some questions.

"Hey," Lydia greets me, her blonde hair falling past her shoulders in loose waves.

I slip through the crack of the door, ignoring the face she makes as I close it behind me. "What can I help you with?"

She blinks a couple of times, still staring at the now-closed off entrance to the cave. "I..."

"You...?" I catch a whiff of her jasmine vanilla perfume and breathe it in as I wait for her to say something. "I know you walked up here for some reason, Lydia."

She nods, her eyes dropping to her feet for a moment and then back up to mine. "There are people outside putting up a fence."

I shrug. "Yes. I hired them to do that. I said I would."

Her brows furrow. "Why?"

"It'll make things easier for you and your dog."

"His name is Duke."

"Okay, for you and *Duke*." I give her a terse smile and head toward the stairs, hoping she'll follow. I don't have a rule about her coming up here, but I'd rather she not. There're too many truths that could come out, and my career is the least of them.

"Can you take the cost of the fence out of my pay?" Lydia's footsteps chase after me. "I don't want it to set you back."

"You're not setting me back, and no, I won't," I say, keeping my eyes focused as I make it to the kitchen. The sun is setting already, and so I guess it's time we discuss the book she's supposed to be writing. I reach into the cabinet above the stainless-steel fridge and retrieve a bottle of scotch and two glasses.

"I don't drink."

I stop as I unscrew the cap. "Interesting."

Lydia's teeth dig into the flesh of her bottom lip as she watches me, as if I'm going to ask her *why* she doesn't drink. "It makes me feel terrible."

"It makes a lot of people feel terrible," I chuckle, swallowing a mouthful of the burning liquid. I leave the second glass empty, making a mental note to never offer her some again.

"It messes with my blood sugar."

"Are you diabetic?"

She wrinkles her nose at me. "Um, no. I'm not. That was all they could come up with. I went to the hospital when I was eighteen, a freshman in college."

"Hmm." I purse my lips as I refill my glass. "You didn't drink until you were eighteen?"

She meets my gaze as I lift my glass, placing it to my lips. "No, I didn't. My parents were strict. I had it in my head that I could try out partying when I went to college. As it turns out, I was born to be a designated driver."

I chuckle again, and her soft pink lips curl into a smile. "I bet your friends appreciated that."

"They did at the time, probably. But I don't seem to keep friends for very long—except Emma. But I didn't meet her until I was twenty-six."

*She's an open book.*

And I fucking love it. I can appreciate the openness of someone, especially when I'm the polar opposite. Though, for Lydia, I might change. Eventually.

"Why don't you keep friends?" I lean against the counter as Lydia's eyes stayed glued to me. I run my gaze over her body, taking in her black baggy T-shirt and pale legs clad in a pair of mid-thigh denim shorts. She's a modest girl—and I can appreciate that.

But for me, she won't be allowed to be.

A blush grows across her cheeks and visibly, her quads grow taught, her muscles tensing. Her finger trails down the white granite as she takes a deep breath, her eyes moving away and flickering to the backyard. The wrought iron picket fence I had installed today is done, and she stares as the men pack up their things.

"Well?" I quip, folding my arms across my chest.

"Sorry," she whips her head back to me, the crimson hue even deeper than before. "It's just a beautiful fence. It pairs well with the house."

I nod, fighting the urge to touch her, force her attention to remain on me. "So, why don't you have friends?"

"I'm terrible at maintaining relationships, I guess," she laughs lightly, and then sighs. "I always forget to text people back and sometimes it's easier to stay home than it is to go somewhere."

"I get that. If it weren't for work, I don't know how often I'd leave."

She nods and hesitates, her demeanor tensing. "I'll go grab my notebook. I should've came prepared."

*Right. Because this is a business meeting.*

I watch her walk away, transfixed on the soft curve of her ass, the fullness of her thighs, and the way her hips gently sway as she makes her way to her room. I'm fully intending to keep this meeting short and move on to the real reason why I brought her here. The patter of Duke's paws draws my attention away, and I turn to see the dog, coming in to get a drink of water from his bowl.

"You've settled in quickly," I tell him.

Duke looks up at me, tilting his head and wagging his tail.

I smile. He's growing on me.

# Eighteen

## Lydia

My hands shake as I pick up my notebook. Henry's mere presence has my body aching in a way I haven't felt in a long time—maybe ever? I shiver as I recall the way his eyes trickled over me, drinking in every inch. Of course, maybe he's just that intense? Maybe that's how he looks at everyone?

I don't know, but the initial fear I felt when we first met is wearing off, though I'm not sure if that's because I've decided he's *not* terrifying, or I've just come to the conclusion that being here is better than being home.

Even if Mason isn't around.

Pushing the thought of my ex away, I swoop up my papers and head back to the kitchen, noticing Duke standing at the door. I peer out, and seeing that the contractors are gone, I open the door for him to go and explore. He sprints out, forgetting I exist as his nose touches the ground. Typical.

"Well, what do you have for me?" Henry's voice comes from behind me.

"Um, so, your only notes were *stalker, jealousy,* and *assassin,*" I read off the words at the top of my page. "And you didn't mention anything about romance, but I was thinking there could be a subplot with that."

"Naturally." He continues to lean against the counter, his glass gripped in his hand. I'm pretty sure it's empty.

"And so I thought that if you wanted a dark thriller, the main character could *be* an assassin—and he can either stalk his victims or maybe he's the one being stalked."

"I like the latter."

"Me, too." I grin. "And then we can give him a love interest that's in some way related to the stalker..."

"Or she could be the stalker."

I raise my brows. "But then he'd have to kill her."

"Not necessarily. Maybe he accepts it...Maybe he *likes* it."

"Okay," I draw out the vowel sound in the word, my heart flipflopping at his teasing tone. "I can work on that. I'll put together a synopsis with that idea and then make a chapter outline for you to approve of."

"You don't have to have my approval. Just go with it."

I shake my head, setting my notebook down on the island. "I always request approval before starting."

"And I'm giving it to you." He sets the glass down and takes a step toward me. My breath hitches, and a smirk forms on his perfectly shaped mouth. "Do I make you nervous, Lydia?"

*Holy shit.*

"Um..."

He crowds me then, placing a hand on either side of me. "*Um* isn't really an answer."

I can smell hints of scotch on his breath, but his cologne is much more potent, the mix of the two intoxicating. "You do."

"You're so honest," he breathes out, one of his hands lifting from the counter to brush my hair behind my ear. His fingers are like fire on my skin, and the room feels devoid of oxygen as they pull away.

"I should...I should probably..." The words escape me as he cocks a brow. I can barely breathe as Henry leans in, his hot breath tickling my ear in a way that runs all the way to my core.

"You should probably stay right here," he growls in a low tone.

A part of me wants to duck and dodge and slip away from him. But the primal, risky woman in me wants to see how far he'll go. And after everything I've been through in the last few days...

I turn my head, brushing my nose against his, our gaze locking. His irises are stormy again, and I challenge him with everything I can muster. Forget professionalism.

"There's no going back from this." His words sound distant as he leans in, brushing his mouth against mine.

I hesitate, squeezing my eyes shut. I haven't kissed someone new in six years, and the thought sends a wave of nerves through my body. But then I feel the burn of his touch, his fingers threading through my hair. Henry's lips press against mine, urging, beckoning...

And I let him in.

A deep, unfamiliar groan comes from his throat as he pins me against the island. His teeth latch onto my bottom lip and tug, and I whimper from the pain. It's fleeting, however, replaced instantly with a surge of primal arousal as I taste the copper filling my mouth. The blood mixes with our tongues, and he grips me tighter, devouring my mouth.

My senses slip as I become desperate for air. I press against his hand, trying to pull myself away. But he keeps me restrained, draining the oxygen from me. My hands fly up in defense, pressing against his chest.

And he finally breaks our kiss.

I suck in as deeply as I can, my head light. His lips stay parted, eyes dilated as his thumb swipes just below my lip.

"You're so fucking beautiful with blood on your face."

I blink a couple of times, my gaze dropping to his thumb, smeared with red. I reach up to my face, running my fingers across my lips, but when I pull it away, there's nothing there.

"I got it all." His voice is husky as his eyes drop to his thumb.

And then he sticks it in his mouth.

My eyes widen as I take in his tongue removing my blood from his skin, and the way it turns me on is...*so wrong*.

Henry chuckles darkly at me. "You have no idea what you just did. You're mine now, Lydia."

My brows shoot up. *Over a kiss? What was it, a blood oath?* I'm at a loss for words as a chill runs down my spine.

"You let me in," he continues, his fingers trailing across my jaw. They work their way down, before wrapping around my throat lightly. His eyes drop to his grip and then back to my gaze, his irises stormy. "You'll never get me out."

I swallow hard. I believe him, but as much as his words sound like a threat, I want more—I want to know what being with someone as intense as Henry feels like. And as if he can sense it, a smirk flashes across his face...

Then he's on me again.

In a whir, my body lifts from the ground, and my ass crashes against the granite counter. His fingers rip the waist of my shorts free, and the force of his tug drops me to my back. Pain sears down my spine from the impact, but all I can feel is *him*. Henry slips everything from my lower half off, dropping it to the floor. I cry out as he drags me across the cool surface, wrapping his arms around my upper thighs.

A strange, new sensation of excitement thrums through my body, and I tense with anticipation. Maybe I should fight him, but I find myself wanting him more than ever. It feels like jumping out of plane, a rush of adrenaline pulsing through me and pooling...right between my legs.

"I don't do things softly," he says huskily as I tip my head up to peer up at him, situated between my legs. I expect him to undo his jeans. But instead, he lowers, his mouth inches from my pussy. I brace, my legs trembling as Henry kisses my inner thigh, sucking the skin into his mouth.

I squirm as pain shoots down my leg, but as soon as it becomes unbearable, he releases, his tongue circling the sore spot. I breathe out in relief, but he's unphased by my reaction, his tongue connecting with my pussy.

"*Ooh*," I pant, as he tastes me, his dark growl vibrating against me.

"You're so sweet, aren't you, Lydia? I hate to break you." He sucks my clit into his mouth, and my back arches as the sensation grows sharp.

I want to scream for him to stop, but the only sound that leaves my mouth is a loud, raw moan as the pain shifts to arousal. It serves to only fuel him more, his grip on my legs growing tighter. My circulation has to be cut off, but my head is hazy as my hips start to move against him.

"That's it," he groans as he sucks me into his mouth again. I shiver and shake as I grow closer to my orgasm. "Be a good girl and come for me."

I squeeze my eyes shut as his tongue buries inside of me, his words sending me right over the edge. An orgasm ravages me, my moans turning to cries as I grasp for him, my nails connecting with the skin of his forearms, and digging in.

He groans as he laps up every drop before his mouth leaves. I shiver at the cool air hitting my bare lower half, and my eyes flutter open as the pleasure resides, a throbbing discomfort suddenly present in place of arousal.

I shoot upward, and Henry catches me by the throat, leaning in and brushing his lips against mine. I try to deepen the kiss, but he tightens his grip and leans away.

"I think that's enough for tonight."

"...Why?" I choke out, my hands flying up to his wrist. Did I do something wrong? Did I come too fast? Maybe I wasn't as good as what he thought I'd be. I have no idea, and it's actually mortifying.

"Your lip is swelling." He releases his fingers and pulls his wrist from my grip. Henry leans over and picks up my shorts and underwear, handing them to me.

I swallow hard, still feeling embarrassed as I watch him round the island and open the lower freezer of the refrigerator. I inch off the counter, the discomfort becoming more intense as I slide off and land on my feet. I pull on my underwear and shorts in a rush, as he comes back with an icepack wrapped in a towel.

"It's really not that bad," I mumble as he leans over me, pressing it to my bottom lip.

"This will help bring down the swelling, though." His eyes focus on my mouth for a few beats before flicking back up. "If I hurt you, it's my job to heal you."

*That sounds toxic.*

But I don't say that. Instead, I nod. I don't *want* to be hurt—unless it's in the way he just did. Then I think I'm okay with it.

And for a vanilla girl like me, that's terrifying.

# Nineteen

## Henry

I've done enough damage for one night.

And I hate myself for it now that Lydia's babying her bottom lip with an icepack. Her hair's a mess, her eyes glistening. But at the same time, she's more breathtaking than ever. I didn't intend to do more than kiss her, but those jade irises beckoned me. I don't think I can tell the woman no, and the fact she has so much power over me already is panic worthy.

"It's really not a big deal." She eyes me, her voice muffled by the icepack against her mouth.

I shake my head at her. "It'll only get worse, Lydia." Her eyes widen and the fear filling her expression has me cringing. I'm so fucking tired of being scary.

"Like at any time? Or..."

"I won't get angry and hurt you. I'd never lay a hand on you in that way," I tell her. I've never taken my anger out on anyone but myself, anyway. Even targets don't get my rage. That's unleashing something I can't come back from. "You just bring out an urge in me to painfully bring you pleasure."

"I liked it."

"That's a dangerous thing to admit," I tell her, breathing out heavily.

She shrugs. The woman who avoided my deal *shrugs* at the idea of me hurting her between the sheets. It's torturous. "I've never done anything *different*."

I stiffen. "I don't want to know that."

She tilts her head. "Why?"

"Because whoever came before me won't exist in your mind when I'm finished with you." *Which will be never.* But I don't want her to know that...yet.

She's silent for a few moments, removing the icepack from her mouth and touching the cool skin with two of her fingers. "Did you want this from me before I came here?"

"Yes."

Her breath catches, her gaze dropping to the icepack resting in her lap. I watch her curiously, trying to decipher the emotions oozing from her expression. I take a step toward her, and her eyes lift instantly, meeting mine.

And I hate what I see.

*Disappointment.*

"What's wrong with me wanting you?" I mean, other than the obvious reasons that she's completely oblivious to right now.

Her lips purse and she winces. "I was engaged."

"I saw the ring."

"I broke up with him right after we met." Her eyes hold mine, and something that I thought was dead and gone comes to life in my chest. "We were together for six years."

"That's a long time to be miserable."

She laughs, devoid of humor. "Something like that."

"Why'd you break up?" I ask, filling my glass with scotch again. My dick is unsatisfied with tonight, but my soul is on a whole other level. She's letting me in. No one lets me in—and for good reason.

She fidgets with the white towel wrapped around the icepack, and then shrugs. "I...I guess it's because he told me he would be fine with me sleeping with you for more money— but it's more than that."

I hate talking about this failure of a man, but if it means we don't have to ever again, then good riddance. "It's fucked up he was supportive of that." Not for me, but for her. She deserves someone who'd never put a price on her.

"He saw it as a way to pay off his student loans," she scoffs, tipping her head back and letting out an empty, painful laugh. Lydia stops then, looking at me. "I don't even miss him. I think I'm messed up, because after *six freaking years*, I'm not heartbroken. And what? A few days later, I'm with someone else, not even thinking about him."

"But you're thinking about him now," I level, downing the rest of the alcohol. I can't blame her for it—it's fresh. But I like to kill and forget about it. It never serves me to relive it.

"Not in that way," she meets my gaze. "He didn't take the breakup well."

*Here we go.*

"Yeah? Well, I figure being dumped by you would be life shattering."

She chuckles. "No, I think it just made him angry. He started stalking me."

I tap my finger on the glass, eyeing her. "Guess it's a good thing you're gone."

"My mom said he took off to Vermont after I left or something. Maybe the cops scared him off." She says the words with a false air of confidence, and it makes my stomach sick.

I could lay it out for her. I could tell her the truth. I could admit that I slit his fucking throat in the name of her, *for* her. He'd never touch her ever again. No one will but me. But she'd hate me—and I don't think I could handle that yet.

"Sorry for unloading," she clears her throat, offering out the icepack. "Talk about a mood killer."

"I told you not to apologize." I take it from her, meeting her eyes. "You'll never kill the mood for me either."

A blush crawls across her cheeks. "I don't know. I can be a lot."

I run my thumb along her bottom lip. "So can I."

A scraping at the door startles her, and she jerks her head around, Duke standing at the glass door, peering in. "Oh my gosh, I forgot he was out there." Lydia slips away from me, trotting to the door and opening it. "I'm so sorry, Dukey." She drops to her knees and hugs the dog.

"I don't think he minded," I tell her, tossing the icepack back into the freezer drawer.

She looks back at me, a playful expression on her face. "Of course, you'd say that."

"It is what it is." I flip the towel over my shoulder, the sound of footsteps catching my attention. Jude appears in the kitchen moments later, his gaze bouncing from me to Lydia. I have no idea if he heard us.

But I don't care.

"Can I talk to you? It's business."

I look to Lydia, who gives me a soft smile.

"I was actually just thinking of heading to bed." She stands to her feet and pats her leg for Duke to follow her. "I'll see you tomorrow." Her attention is on me, the warmth in her eyes triggering that feeling in my chest again.

"Good night, Lydia." I watch as she disappears from the kitchen, and a few moments later, the sound of a door closing fills the silence. I shift my gaze back to Jude. "What?"

He shakes his head. "You're actually getting to her."

"It's meant to be."

Jude gives me an incredulous expression. "Says who?"

I shrug. "Me."

"Well, here we go," he groans, but then straightens up. "Carlson is on a rampage."

"What?"

"He's destroying his office...And his wife."

"Shit. Keep an eye on Lydia."

# Twenty

## Lydia

I heard Henry leave nearly thirty minutes ago, not long after Jude appeared in the kitchen. But who leaves for work at this time? Aren't they just in tech? I shake my head and roll over in bed, my face down in the pillow. The sting of my lip has long faded, though between my legs is still slightly sore.

And it's a strangely sweet reminder that he was there.

He still scares me, but it's now laced with excitement and intrigue. I want to know who he is, and there's a nagging feeling in my gut there's a lot more to him. I push myself up on my elbows and reach for my phone. I unlock the screen, hoping to see a text from Emma, letting me know she made it.

But there's none.

I send her a quick message, asking how she's doing, and then sit up, pulling my knees up underneath me. Duke is sleeping soundly on the bed, and I give him a pat before slipping out of bed, phone in hand. For all I know, Henry could just be running a couple of late-night errands and he'll be back sooner rather than later...

But I'll hear him if that happens.

Besides, Henry told me that if I needed anything, I could come to his room. Now, I need something. I need to know who he is. I pad quietly to the door, opening it silently. I peer out and down the hallway. The curtains are closed, and the house is pitch black. I steady my heart and close the door softly behind me. My eyes flicker to the door at the end of the hall.

*Please don't hate me for this.*

I feel guilty for snooping, but it doesn't stop me. If I'm going to let him touch me—and claim me, apparently—I need to know *who* I'm making this arrangement with. I make it to the solid black door and cast a glance over my shoulder. No one is there.

My hand tries the knob, and it turns. I push the door in and slip inside, shutting it behind me. I blink to adjust to the darkness. His room is nearly twice the size of mine and I click on the flashlight function, shining it across the room. Shelves line the walls, and they're full of books. His king-sized bed sits in the center of the back wall and there's a desk on the only spot without shelving. There're two other doors, which I assume are a closet and bathroom.

I breathe in the heavy scent of him, committing it to memory. I begin to creep around the room, shining the light across the books on his shelves. Most of them are nonfiction, classics, and titles I've never heard of. However, it doesn't take me long to realize that they're listed under alphabetical order by author last name. I can't help it.

I search for my pen name, *Piper Lewis.*

It takes a few minutes, but I *finally* find them. All six of them. They don't belong in the mix of his taste, but there they are. I tug out the first one, flipping through it. It's not annotated. I put it back and move to the next ones, flipping through them until I make it to the last one, which just so happens to be the first one I ever released.

I flip it open, and freeze.

*This is the author I was telling you about. It's not your style, but I swear this guy reminds me of you. Actually, all of the men in her books bring you to mind. It's crazy. -Cher*

Who the hell is Cher? Unwarranted jealousy courses through my veins, and as I flip through the rest of the book, I see a few highlights. I don't read them. I stick it back on the shelf with a frown. Some girl is the reason he started reading my work. *Yuck.*

It shouldn't matter though.

I push it away and continue moving around the room. I pause at the nightstand, tempted to open the drawer, but I don't. The computer on the desk catches my attention first. I creep across the room and open it.

A stock image of a cityscape fills the screen and I squint at the bright light, setting my phone to the side. My index presses the *enter* key, and the option for a password pops up. I purse my lips as I rack my brain.

Nothing comes to mind.

I don't even know his birthday. I don't know *anything* about him, actually. I could count the facts on one hand, yet I'm already feeling myself fall for him. I never can be intimate with someone without developing some sort of stupid attachment. Talk about being careless.

I snap the laptop shut, and pull at the desk drawers, but the sound of a door closing catches my attention. I freeze, listening closely, and then the sound of the sink running fills my ears. I head for the door, cracking it open just enough for me to peer down the hallway. A light illuminates the front room, and I slip out, closing it behind me.

Quietly, I head for my room, but then catch sight of Jude, making a bowl of cereal, and I see my opportunity. I head for the kitchen, and he looks up as I enter.

"It's late," he says flatly.

"I couldn't sleep."

He picks up the white glass bowl full of Cheerios. "I see. There're meals prepped for you in the fridge."

I nod. "I know, I saw them earlier."

"He takes your presence here seriously. He has Lola cook enough for you to be well fed all week—until she comes back to clean and cook."

*Lola?*

"Can I ask you something?"

He sets the bowl down, the spoon clattering against the ceramic. "I can't guarantee I can answer, but sure."

"Who is Cher?"

His brows shoot up. "How'd you find out about her?"

My stomach knots up at the mention. "I saw it in a book on his shelf."

"Why didn't you just ask Henry?"

I shrug. "I didn't want to be weird." *And he wasn't here.*

Jude laughs. "Well, I don't think it'd be very weird to ask him about his sister. She occasionally sends him shit."

"Does she ever come visit?"

"No, but Henry visits her sometimes."

I nod, making a note. "When's his birthday?"

Jude blinks. "Uh...September fourth. He'll be thirty-three this year. Doesn't look it, though. I swear youth hangs onto him."

"Yeah..." I tap my finger against the granite, noticing Jude's bowl of cereal is sitting in the same spot Henry devoured me.

"If you have a lot questions, you should talk to Henry about them. I don't know how much he wants you to know— and pissing him off is not something I care to do."

"Is he dangerous when he gets angry?" It's a stupid but necessary question, considering he told me earlier he'd never hurt me. In *that* way, at least.

Jude takes a bite of cereal, chewing it slowly before swallowing. "He's..." His voice trails off in an unnerving way. "If he says he'll never hurt you, then he won't."

I bite down on my lip, confused. "So he's dangerous?"

Jude lets out a sharp breath. "Isn't everyone? We all are capable of horrible things, Lydia. There are just people who learn to control those urges, those who can't control them, and those who choose to let those urges loose sometimes."

"Which one are you?"

He laughs. "I'd say the first."

I nod, feeling a little bit of relief. "And Henry?"

"The last one."

A shudder rolls down my spine.

"I'll give you some advice." Jude picks his bowl up from the counter. "It's better to go to the source of the answers versus trying to pull the information out of someone else." He slips past me and heads for the exit of the kitchen.

"Wait, Jude," I call after him.

"Yeah?" He glances back at me.

"Where is Henry right now?"

The expression that crosses his face sends my stomach in a twist. "Again, that's a question for him, not me. I have a feeling he'll tell you when he's ready to. Just don't miss the truth in front of your face right now."

I struggle with the riddle he just threw at me as he disappears, leaving me alone in the kitchen. Is he trying to tell me something? Am I really too stupid to see something right in front of my face? I bite down on my sore lip as I return to my room.

I'll just have to ask Henry himself when he shows back up.

# Twenty-One

## Henry

This is bad.

Blood is all over the kitchen floor, and I step around it, careful not to leave any footprints. I hear them upstairs, a struggle ensuing. I move faster. We don't know if the wife scheduled the hit, but if a target kills someone else while *we* are responsible, it's bad for everyone involved.

And it's never happened to me.

I adjust the mask on my face as I race up the stairs, adrenaline pumping through my body. The high of the chase has already started, and I float silently toward the noises coming from the master bedroom. The door is open, and as soon as I reach the threshold, I see Carlson over his wife, his hands wrapped around her throat.

"Fucking bitch!"

She mumbles something back at him, and he rears back, his fist raised. I spring into action, gliding up behind him. My left hand fists the back of his polo as my right guides the knife across his neck. The sharpened blade and force of my attack leaves him nearly decapitated as I shove him off the bed.

*This is a catastrophe.*

"You've got a witness," Jude says in my ear, crunching something obnoxiously. I ignore him and step around Carlson until I make it to his wife—well, *widow*, actually. Her dark hair is smattered with blood, her nose twisted to the side. Bright blue eyes stare at the ceiling fan, not even phased by my mask. In fact, if it weren't for the fact she just blinked her lashes, I'd have thought she was dead.

"Medical attention needed?" Jude asks in my ear.

I don't know. I lean over her, taking in the scrapes and bruises covering her aging skin. There're scars beneath the fresh injuries, and I have a feeling this woman was broken long before this night. I frown beneath the mask, studying her. Her breaths are even, and while I'm certain her nose is probably broken, otherwise, she appears fine.

So, I shake my head.

"Okay, then grab the cameras and get the fuck out of there."

I take one last look at the woman on the bed, my mind flashing to Lydia. Would her putrid ex-fiancé ever have broken her like this?

"Move," Jude snaps in my ear. "Teenager is home."

*Shit.*

I grab the tiny camera from the bedroom and step out, closing the door. As much as I don't want to leave her, it's not abnormal to leave someone clinging to life. However, Mrs. Carlson isn't clinging to life physically...Just in all the other ways.

"She's gone straight to her room, but this is messy."

I breathe out some relief and move through the house, gathering the cameras and sliding them into the pocket of my hoodie. "I can't leave with the body there."

"You have to. The police are going to have to take this one."

"They'll blame the wife," I growl under my breath. "And that's an easy one to believe once you see her in person." I head back for the stairs, knowing I might be making a *huge* mistake.

But I can't forget the thought of Lydia lying there in the woman's place.

*I'll never break Lydia like this.*

I make it back to the bedroom and open the door. The wife is still there on the bed, but she's sitting up now, her arms wrapped around her knees.

"You need to get up and shower," I instruct her.

"Don't do this," Jude warns me. "You need to leave."

I shake my head. "You and your daughter need to go somewhere tonight."

She stares at me, but slowly bobs her head. Her frail body scoots across the bed, and as she stands to her feet, her gray sweats hang loosely on her body. "Thank you."

"Leave the clothes in the room."

She nods, wrapping her arms around herself. "I won't tell anyone."

I don't know if I believe her, but as soon as she's in the bathroom, I rip the comforter off the bed and cover Carlson's body. I wipe my blade across the white material, cleaning it.

"Call for cleanup," I mutter as I slide it into its sheath.

"Okay, I'll have them show up once everyone leaves. Now, *please* get the fuck out of there, Henry. You've damn near exposed yourself."

"Right." I spin on my heels and escape down the stairs. I rip the side door open from the kitchen and trot across the dark lawn. Jude cut off all the outside lights and cameras, but I could still easily be seen. I remove the mask as I slide into the Mercedes. It's going to have to go—and soon. I toss the mask to the passenger seat, and glance back to the house.

I hope like hell they'll keep their mouths shut. I'm putting a lot of weight into the hands of strangers...All because I thought of Lydia in the middle of it.

She's giving me a conscience. And I don't know if that's a good thing.

\*\*\*

I make it back to the house hours later after ditching the car, trading it in for a black Lexus. I cut the engine and tap the close button for the garage. The sun is already rising in the sky, but the warm orange glow is replaced by darkness as the door fully shuts.

And taking a few minutes, I run my hands over my face.

*Holy shit.*

A nagging feeling tugs at my gut, and I can't put my finger on it. I don't try to either. I pull the handle of the driver's side door, the lights in the car kicking on. I'm still wearing my black gloves, and so I pull them off, shoving them into my backpack and slinging it over my shoulder.

*What would Lydia think of me if she knew?*

The question is intrusive, and I push it away. It doesn't matter what she'd think. This is what it is, and I have to get better about separating my obsession with Lydia and work. It makes me weak.

I climb out of the car and exit the garage, climbing the stairs and entering the house. I creep through the mudroom, and the glow of a light catches my attention. The kitchen light is on, and I glance down at myself. There's blood on the shirt beneath my fresh hoodie, soaking the neckline, and I'm sure it's speckled across my face.

As I round the corner, I catch sight of Jude, pouring a cup of coffee. "You look exhausted."

He looks up, dark circles under his eyes. "Long night. I've had to cover a lot of digital footprints, and the cleanup crew has no idea you have a witness. If it gets out you interacted with—"

"We don't have to discuss this any further. I don't know how it would get out."

"Uh, the wife telling the daughter—or just anyone—that some guy came into her house, killed her husband, and then people made it all disappear."

"She'd sound batshit crazy."

"We might operate in the dark part of society, but our techniques are not all that hidden. People are aware of contract killers."

"Yeah, and for all we know she's the one who hired us."

Jude shakes his head, sipping on his coffee. "I don't know. This is the first time you've ever interacted with someone and gone against what I told you to do. We should've left it."

"They would've thought she did it."

"So?" Jude throws a hand up. "So what? It *happens*. It's. Not. Our. Problem. I'm going to have to continue surveillance on them for this."

"I'm too tired to argue with you," I groan, running my fingers through my hair.

His face turns cold. "I just don't know what made you lose it. It's Lydia, isn't it?"

"Don't bring her into this," I warn him. "It's not about Lydia."

"Yeah, it is," he levels with me, his voice stern. "I can tell. So what happened, Henry?" I shake my head. Jude takes a step forward, his face darkening. "*What happened?*"

"Fuck." I rub my burning eyes, riddled with fatigue. "I don't know. I just...I saw the woman lying there, and I couldn't let her take the fall for it. She's shattered, and I just pictured Lydia..."

"I get it." Jude nods, his voice only slightly losing its edge. "And as much as I want to fuck you up over this, there's no point. You need to shower before she gets up. You're covered in blood."

"Yeah," I mutter. I slip past him and head for my room. I don't even stop to listen when I pass Lydia's door. She doesn't need to see me in this state. It'd be more shocking than just telling her the truth. I enter my room, flip the light on, and tuck my backpack away in the closet.

My room is my safe haven, but as I strip down and start to shower, it doesn't feel that way. No, things are shifting, and I'm starting to think *Lydia* is replacing it. She has no idea how strongly I feel pulled to her.

And as I step out of the shower and towel dry, the urge to be with her grows. I pull on a pair of sweatpants and head down the hallway. Jude is still in the kitchen, mindlessly staring out the open windows. Something about last night really bothered him.

But he'll get over it.

I reach for the doorknob and my mind flashes back to Lydia's house, the first time I entered. The thought leaves me excited and aroused. She had no idea I was there, but now, she's at *my* house. At *my* disposal.

But I'll never dispose of her.

My fingers turn the knob, and I press the door in. Duke greets me, his tail wagging as he jumps from the bed and bounds through the opening. Jude can let him out. I close the door behind me, my gaze focused on Lydia, laying there peacefully. She's facing the edge of the bed.

And the need for her swells in my body.

I walk around to the other side of the bed and flip the covers back, crawling in beside her. I don't care if it's too fast. I don't care if it startles her. My hand slides beneath her, and I drag her into my chest, her ass pressed against my cock.

She mumbles something sleepily as my fingers trace the bare skin of her hip. She's wearing just an oversized T-shirt and a thin pair of underwear, and I slip my hand under the material of her shirt, not stopping until I connect with the soft flesh of her breast. I squeeze the handful hard enough that she squirms, but as her ass rubs me, she finds rhythm, a light moan slipping from her lips.

"Good girl," I murmur in her ear, brushing her mess of blonde hair out of the way with my nose. I plant a kiss on her neck, sucking her skin hard enough to leave a mark. I want this woman covered in me. Lydia moans, her eyes fluttering open as my fingers trail down her stomach, disappearing into her underwear.

*Fuck, she's so wet.*

I growl into her skin as my fingers dive into her slits, her moisture covering my hand. She bucks her hips against me as her head turns, catching my gaze. Her lips part as though she might say something, but I push two fingers deep inside of her. Lydia's face contorts with pleasure, but I need more from her this morning.

I remove my hands from her and go for the end of her T-shirt, pulling it up and over her head. She doesn't fight me as she lands on her back. Instead, her green eyes rake over my bare chest, reading across it like the inked pictures on my skin are a page in a book.

Her fingers brush across me as I toss her shirt to the floor, leaving goosebumps in their wake. My eyes take her in, her body baring her small, perky breasts for the first time. Her pink nipples stand erect, and I dip down to one, sucking it into my mouth.

And just like always, I'm never gentle.

"*Ooh!*" she cries out, her back arching as I bite down on her and then lap the pain away with my tongue. "*Henry.*" My name comes out of her mouth like she's in a trance.

And I nearly explode at the sound.

I rip the material of her underwear and rid myself of my sweats. My cock is throbbing. "I fucking need you, Lydia." The words come out of my mouth in a heady rasp of desire, and I force her legs apart.

Her breath is sharp as I press into her, my eyes nearly rolling back into my head as I enter the tight, warm, and wet place. A whimper slips from her lips as our eyes lock, and I fill her the rest of the way.

"You feel so good," I groan, falling forward. I rest with a fisted hand on either side of her head as I pump in and out, ridding my mind of the events of last night—of the woman lying broken on the bed.

# Twenty-Two

## Lydia

*Holy...*

My mind feels hazy as Henry fucks me, the weight of his body coming down on mine. I grab for him, my fingernails digging into the inked snake wrapping around a skull on his chest. His eyes are dark and hooded but fixated on my face rather than his cock ravaging me. I never thought I'd wake up to this, and I never knew I'd enjoy it so much.

Pleasure builds in my core as he thrusts, every stroke hitting something the right way deep inside of me. His right hand lifts from beside my head as he suddenly slows, his thumb running along my lower lip.

"Will you trust me?" The words come out low and in almost a growl as he presses his thumb into my mouth.

Innately, as if I've done it a thousand times before, I suck his thumb. His pupils dilate, and I find myself nodding in response to his question. I'll consider the real answer later—when I'm not on the edge of an orgasm.

Henry's expression grows dark, pulling his hand from my face. His hips still, leaving himself lodged deep inside of me, but unmoving. I brace as his fingers glide across my jaw, leaving goosebumps in their wake...

And then wrap around my throat.

"Tell me to stop, and I'll try. "

*He'll try?*

I squeak out a sound, but he squeezes, cutting off my air supply.

"If you can't speak then tap my arm twice," he continues, leaning down and brushing his lips to mine. Finally. Ever since I woke up to him in my bed, I wanted him to kiss me.

Though I can't exactly kiss him back right now.

I manage to part my lips, and he loosens his grip, letting me have air as he devours my mouth. Arousal floods my system as I taste him again, and the forbidden act of playing with my life might be the biggest turn on I've ever felt. He has so much power, and yet, *I* feel empowered. His hips begin to move again, and my need to come rises back like it never faded. Henry pulls his lips from mine, his face darkening as he begins to squeeze my throat...

And the dance begins.

He thrusts his cock into me, the momentum behind his body increasing. My hips rock with him, building my own pleasure. But as I gasp for air, his fingers dig into my skin, cutting off my supply. My eyes widen as my head begins to go light, but then feel a strong urge to close. My vision begins to go, blurring with Henry above me, his troubled eyes icier than ever. And just as I reach up to tap him, he releases, letting me fill my lungs greedily with air.

Arousal pours to my pussy, and suddenly I orgasm, a warm sensation rolling through my body.

"*Henry!*" I cry out, my eyes growing wet as his force only increases. I pulse around him, and he sucks in a sharp breath. His body tenses, shuddering as he lets out a groan, coming inside of me.

"Such a good girl," he murmurs, leaning over me and giving me a light kiss. He releases my throat, and my hands fly up where his just was, raking over the spot.

*Is this going to bruise?*

I swallow, expecting to feel pain, but there is none. In fact, I don't feel any discomfort at all—on my throat anyway. As he pulls out, there is an ache between my legs, but I'm not sure if it's because I want him to fill me again—or because he fucked me harder than I've ever been before.

My eyes stay glued to him as he grabs his pants, and then eases them up over his hips. "Where did you go last night?" I blurt the words out before I can stop myself.

"Work."

I purse my lips, hating the answer. That's *not* a real answer, and anger builds in my chest. Without saying anything, I reach over and grab my shirt, pulling it over my head.

"What's wrong?" he calls after me as I climb out of bed, ignoring his gaze. I head straight for the bathroom and turn on the shower. It's amazing how fast incredible sex can turn into a mixture of overwhelming and unwanted emotions.

"Lydia," Henry's voice turns sharp as he whips open the bathroom door. His eyes rake over my naked body as I strip off the T-shirt. I don't even know why I put it back on in the first place, but whatever.

"Can you not stare at me?" I snap at him as I grab for a towel.

"No," he shoots back, stopping my hand before it reaches the soft, gray material. "You're going to tell me why you're suddenly pissed off at me."

I raise my brows. "What even makes you think I'm *pissed off*? I just want to shower." I turn my back to him and step in under the water, ignoring the sharp sigh that leaves his lips.

"I know I can be rough," his voice cuts through the glass door, groveling in his tone. I can see his figure leaning against the wall just outside, and I hope his view in is as hazy as my view out. "You can always stop me."

"It's not about that." I shake my head out of frustration as I reach for the shampoo. "I just don't believe you."

"Believe me?"

"I don't think you were just *at work* last night," I finally admit, feeling stupid for even caring. I've only been here a couple of days, and I'm getting wrapped up in emotions like a lovesick teenager—but Henry brings it out of me. When he doesn't respond, I keep going. "If you work in tech, why would you be gone all night long? Is it customer service? And why is Jude so weird about telling me anything?"

The shower door rips open, and Henry's face is stone cold. "I *was* working last night."

I swallow hard, gathering my courage. I never challenged Mason, and now, I know that was a huge mistake. "What kind of work were you doing then? Because there's not that many types of tech businesses that stay open all night—"

"You're really going to keep questioning me?" His tone shifts to threatening as the shampoo finishes rinsing from my hair. He steps into the shower, and I suddenly recall the fear I felt the first day I met him. "What do *you* think I was doing last night, Lydia? Fucking someone else?"

My mouth gapes because I'd never admit it—but maybe I *was* worried about that. "I...I don't..."

Henry crowds me, pinning my body against the wall. He grabs my chin, forcing my eyes to his but keeping the grip light. "I will *never* fuck someone else. Think what you want about me, but I belong to you—whether you want me or not."

My chest heaves as he drops his hand from my face. His words are overwhelming. Is he really falling for me this fast? Isn't this bad? His gaze drifts from mine and Henry turns, exiting the shower and shutting the door. I stare after him, the warm water suddenly feeling cold on my skin. I shiver, shutting it off and stepping out. I wrap a towel around my body, hugging myself.

No one has ever belonged to me, and I'm not sure if I should be excited or freaking terrified.

***

I don't see Henry the rest of the day. I spend it working on the plot, attempting to hash something out as my mind churns with confusion. I've always been a people pleaser, and I know that if it were to get out that I'm sleeping with Henry—a client and borderline stranger—everyone would think I was crazy...

Or a slut.

I cringe at the word, memories coming back to mind. There's a reason I had to move away from my hometown— even by just an hour. I hadn't even done anything, but mean girls do mean girl things. And even my own parents thought I slept around.

But unbeknownst to them, I've only ever been with Mason—and now Henry. Mason *never* got my body to react in the same way Henry does, though...

He didn't choke me, either.

For some reason that thought makes me laugh, and I set my pen down on the desk. I push back from it, my eyes casting over the story I've plotted out. Something about it feels off...I've followed Henry's thoughts and ideas, but still. It just seems like it's missing the mark.

I rub my eyes and decide to leave it for a while. I'm sore from this morning, but don't let it show as I leave my room, scanning the house for signs of Duke. He's wanted outside constantly since the fence has gone up and I don't blame him. It's warm and sunny, the opposite of what it's like back at home right now.

The house is eerily silent, and it gives me even more of an urge to get out and take Duke for a walk. I grab the harness and leash, slip out the door, and search for Duke. He hears me, and comes running from the far-right corner, his tail wagging.

"Let's go, boy." I give him the sit command with my hand and fasten the harness to his wriggling body. He walks politely beside me as we make our way to the gate on the far end of the yard. "What a strange day."

I breathe in the salty air and let the sun warm my skin as my bare feet smoosh the sand between my toes. I head to the water, but don't wade in, only letting it wash the sand away temporarily. Then, I peer down the beach, which appears to be mostly empty aside from some umbrellas and beachgoers in lounge chairs beneath them.

"Be a good dog," I warn Duke as we head off down the shoreline. I pull my phone from my denim shorts pocket, frustrated that I *still* haven't heard from Emma.

*What the hell?*

I scroll to her contact and pull up her name, hitting the call button and putting it to my ear. She was supposed to be here already. It rings three times, and then goes to voicemail. Frustrated, I hang up and try again.

"Hey," Emma answers on the second ring.

I let out a sigh of relief. "Where have you been? I haven't heard from you. Are you out here yet?"

Silence.

"Um, actually, I haven't left yet," her voice drops. "I'm hoping to leave soon though. I just..."

"It's Jared, isn't it?"

"You know how he can be."

"Yeah," I say through gritted teeth. "You should just leave him and come anyway, Em. You don't have to let him lord over you. He signed a prenup."

She sighs. "I don't know. It's not that easy."

"Emma..." I want to argue with her, tell her to just pack a bag and fly across the country to join me. She's part of the reason that I gave this place a chance, and while Henry might be mysterious and sometimes frightening, he's much better than living in fear of Mason.

Plus this view? I cast my eyes across the blue waves and glimmering waters. It's par none.

"I'm figuring it out," Emma tells me, her voice low. "And I'm sorry I didn't make it, Lydia. I thought he wouldn't care, but he did."

"It's okay. I understand."

"How're things there though?" Her voice lifts the way it always does when we change the subject. She's closed off most of the time, and I wish I lived closer so I could show up and see for myself.

"They're fine," I tell her blankly, walking behind Duke. "Things have um...escalated. Again. In a different way."

"Uh, *what?*" Emma bursts into a fit of giggles that eases my worries about her. "You mean you slept with him, right? Please tell me you did and it's not more stalker problems."

"I did." My cheeks grow hot.

"Oh my gosh, that's incredible. What a way to stick it to Mason. I'm so proud of you for getting out there and living a little."

"Thanks," I mutter, glancing back to the house. "I'm just trying to not...Um..."

"Catch feelings?"

I make a face. "I guess. I should know better by now to let it be, but things are *intense* between us."

"Gotta love some sexual chemistry."

"Yeah..." My voice trails off as my phone begins to beep in my ear. "Hang on." I pull it away, surprised to see my mother calling me. Again. I ignore it. "Sorry."

"It's fine, so what's he like?"

"He's difficult to read," I admit. "But he's made his interest in me clear—and that's about the only thing he's made clear."

"Ooh girl," she giggles as my phone vibrates against my ear again. I pull it away from my ear, this time seeing a message.

> Mason is missing! Call me!

My heart drops at the message, a cold chill running through my body despite the warming of the sun. "I gotta go," I tell Emma blankly. "I'll call you later." I hang up before she can say anything. Something feels *all* wrong in the moment, my head going light as I replay the events of the last few days.

But I can't put my finger on it.

I mean, maybe I'd fallen out of love with Mason, but the news of him going missing *for real* is still shocking. I stop Duke and go to the browser on my phone, typing in *Mason Prewitt.*

Multiple articles pop up from both Vermont *and* Oklahoma. I click the first one, pouring over the words.

*Oklahoma man now considered missing and endangered after leaving Jackson's Pool House. Surveillance footage shows the thirty-two-year-old man leaving the bar just past one o'clock in the morning with an unidentified male.*

I blink at the grainy footage, struggling to make out the picture shown. My heart pounds as I watch the video embedded in the article. My stomach churns, bile rising in my throat as I watch my ex-fiancé walk out of the bar and then disappear into oblivion.

# Twenty-Three

## Henry

"That's some really good footage manipulation," I muse as I peer over Jude's shoulder, taking in the sight of AI generated Mason leaving the bar.

"It's wild, because there's even witnesses saying they saw him there." Jude looks over at me, grinning. "Mad what people think they remember based off a completely fake video."

I bob my head and lean back in the chair. "People can be manipulated to believe anything when the right person is doing it."

"Like you and Lydia."

I glare at him. "No. I'm not manipulating her, I'm just not telling her all of the truth. My intention with her is..." I stop myself from saying *good*, because I don't know that I ever have *good* intentions with anything—though this last hit has me questioning my cold-bloodedness. And speaking of... "Have you caught any movement from the widow and daughters?"

"No, but we got paid this morning." His voice drops as he looks over at me. "And hopefully, they stay quiet about it. Nothing has hit the news about his death, but I don't know if I should even try to manipulate anything to make it out like he ran off. I never tamper when there're witnesses. We let the police handle it and we go dark."

I tense my jaw, that nagging gut feeling returning. "It'll be fine. Assholes go missing all the time. And like I said, for all we know, the wife called the hit."

"But we *don't* know that for sure," Jude argues.

"Fuck, man, let it go," I rumble. "We'll deal with it if something comes of it. There's no point in worrying over it now. It's a waste of time."

Jude exhales sharply but doesn't push. "Lydia is downstairs making her dinner." He pulls up the security camera in the kitchen and nods as Lydia pulls out one of the already-made dinners. "If you're going to do this right, it might be nice for her to not eat alone every night. Don't just show up and fuck her. Women don't like that."

I blink a couple of times and stand to my feet. "Since when do you know anything about women?"

He chuckles. "I don't know shit, but I do know that."

"Thanks for the info." I roll my shoulders and head downstairs, making quick work of the distance. By the time I make it to the kitchen, Lydia is sliding onto a bar stool, her fork hovering over the broccoli and cheese stuffed chicken and rice.

"Hey," I greet her.

Her eyes don't move from the fork. "Hey."

*Well, this is awkward.*

"You wanna go out for dinner or something?" I'm pretty sure I sound as weird as I feel in the moment, but it gets her attention at least.

Lydia lifts her head. "Go out for dinner?"

"Uh, yeah," I chuckle, folding my arms across my chest. "Isn't that what people do who are together?"

Her eyes narrow. "So we're together?"

"Why are you questioning every word that comes out of my mouth, Lydia? I fucked you. We're *together.*"

"Like a fling."

What. The. Hell.

"No. I don't do *flings*. Not with you."

"Good to know," she snorts, shaking her head. She stabs the fork violently into a piece of chicken, lifting it to her mouth. However, just as I think she's about to take a bite, she drops it back down. "I'm not hungry."

"So you don't want to go out?"

"No," she says flatly, sliding off the stool. "Whoever cooks all your food is great, though. Better than eating out." Lydia picks up the glass Tupperware lid and places it back on the container.

"Is this about earlier?"

She glances over at me and goes to the fridge, placing the meal back on the shelf. "No, it's not about earlier."

"So, what's it about then?"

"I think I'm gonna go to bed." She passes by me, but I grab her arm.

"You're not leaving this room without telling me what the hell is going on in that beautiful head of yours."

She rolls her eyes. "Stop it."

Irritation burns in my chest. "Stop what? Caring about you? Yeah, that's not gonna happen, Lydia."

Her shoulders slump. "You don't even know me."

"I do know you."

"No, you know the books I've written. That's not me."

"It's a window to you." *And I've peered through all of yours.*

"It's not!" She throws her hands up, her bare stomach exposed momentarily. I have to force my eyes upward to keep my thoughts in line. "I'm a storyteller—and not even a great one at that. It's all *fiction*. My life is a *mess* right now."

"Now we're getting somewhere." I tug her into me. "Keep going, baby."

Her jaw drops. "Did you—why did you just call me *baby?*"

"I'm sorry, would you prefer something else? Maybe stubborn-ass beautiful? Thick-skulled precious?"

She almost cracks a smile at me. "No."

"So tell me, darling, what is on your mind?" I brush my nose against hers, and she lets out a sigh, her eyes closing and body relaxing.

But then those jade eyes flutter open. "My ex-fiancé is 'missing."

Rage. I feel *rage.*

"I see" is all I can mutter. And it's emotionless. *Why does she care? He was going to hurt her. He was berating her. He was a worthless, piece of shit human being.*

"It's just shocking," she continues, her expression finally breaking to show the grief...and *fear*. "I hope he turns up and nothing bad has happened to him."

*Well, that's not gonna happen.*

"I think he was super messed up over us splitting up—and he lost it on me—but I wouldn't wish harm on anyone. Maybe prison," she laughs dryly. "But not death. I don't wish for anyone to die."

"No one?"

She studies my face. "I don't know. Maybe. Maybe some people deserve it."

I nod. I don't know what else to do. I can't offer an apology I don't mean. I'm not sorry Mason is gone. I've killed more people than there are days in a calendar year on top of that. It's what made me a man—a fucked up one, nonetheless.

"Are you busy tonight?" Her question draws me out of the bleak thought and back to the freckles splashed over the bridge of her nose.

"No, I don't think so."

She turns her wrist in my grip, her fingers lacing around my skin and gripping me back. "Come with me."

I let her lead. My eyes spot Duke curled up on the couch, and he watches us as we head down the hallway. She turns the doorknob of her room, but I stop her.

"I want you in my bed tonight."

She looks up at me and releases the doorknob. "Okay," she breathes out. "But what about Duke?"

"I'll get him later."

She audibly swallows and it goes straight to my dick. Lydia thinks she knows what's coming—but she really has no idea. I don't want to just fuck her. I want to try to love her. I want to fucking love her.

But I don't know if I can.

I close the door behind us and lock it. I position her in front of me, my heart pounding in my ears. My hands reach for the hem of her shirt, and I pull it over her head, her blonde hair falling messily over her shoulders. I take a step toward her. She's tense, her breaths shallow.

I go for her jean shorts next, unbuttoning them, and letting them fall to the floor. My gaze drinks her in, her black bralette and matching underwear contrasting against her creamy skin. I remove my own shirt, and she beats me to my black jeans, unbuttoning them. I ease out of the denim, still transfixed on her.

"Eager," I murmur, meeting her eyes. They're on fire with desire and lust. I want to ravage her, my hands shaking. I want my hand wrapped around her throat again, making her come by stealing her oxygen...

But as we shed each other of the remainder of our clothes, she drops to her knees, not even giving me a chance. She holds my eyes as she leans forward, running her tongue around my tip.

"Oh *fuck*," I groan as she takes me into the warmth of her mouth. I thread my fingers through her hair, pulling it out of her face. She takes me all the way to the back of her throat, her lips encasing my shaft. I'm tempted to hold her there, and gag her, but she starts working back and forth without my help.

"You're too fucking good at this," I pant, as she tips her head back enough to meet my gaze with fire in her eyes.

A smile tugs at her lips, even if they're full of my cock. She lets out a moan of delight as she picks up speed, taking me down her throat. My grip tightens on her hair, and she quickens, drawing me to the edge.

*She wants to fucking please me.*

And that sends me right over the edge. I come in her mouth, holding her head to my cock, not allowing her to back away until I'm done. Only then do I release her. Lydia swallows, and then looks up at me, running her tongue along her bottom lip.

"Get up," I rasp, my cock still hard.

However, as I pull her into me, there's a heavy knock on the door. "What the hell?" I quip, picking up my shirt and tossing it to Lydia. The disturbance fills me with annoyance. "Put that on. In the bathroom. Now." She nods, blushing as she slips off to the open bathroom door.

I unlock the door and rip it open, holding it in a way so Jude *can't* see my dick. "What do you want?" But as soon as the words leave my lips, I can already tell something is all wrong.

"You need to go to Luca. *Now.*"

"Give me a second."

I slam the door in his face, my stomach beginning to churn as I reach for my boxer briefs and jeans. There's never a good reason for me to visit Luca. I get dressed as Lydia appears from the bathroom.

"Is everything okay?" The worry in her face is unsettling.

"Yeah, it's fine." I don't know if that's honest, and for some reason, lying to her now makes me angry. But if she knew the truth...

It'd be over for her.

I open the dresser drawer and pull out another white T- shirt, ignoring the way her eyes follow my every move. I shrug it on and go back to the drawer, pulling my pistol from under my socks. I don't look at her.

"Henry...what...what are you involved in?"

I shake my head. "I can't do this right now." I turn to her, grab her hand, and pull her into me. Threading my fingers through her hair, I give her a hard kiss on the mouth. I'm given a small amount of relief as she kisses me back until I pull away. "I'll see you when I get back."

And with that, I'm out the door, Jude hot on my heels to feed me the news that only happens in my nightmares.

# Twenty-Four

## Lydia

*Where's my phone?*

I search through the pockets of my jean shorts, fishing out the device, and unlocking the screen. I pull up Emma's number and hit the call button.

*Call failed.*

Shaking my head, I try it again, my heart rate picking up in my chest.

Again, the call fails.

"What the hell?" I mumble under my breath as I go to my mom's contact information. I hit the call button...

And it fails, too.

My brow furrows as I look at my signal in the top right-hand corner of the screen. A chill rolls down my spine. There is none. I power my phone down, and then turn it back on, hoping it's just some fluke. Maybe it got wet? But the alarms are going off in my head as I replay the way Henry shoved that gun in the back of his waistband.

As it turns back on, there's still no signal.

I rip Henry's shirt over my head and get dressed in my own clothes. I glance toward the door, and then rush to it, flipping the lock. I turn back around and take in his room in a whole new light. I go straight to his nightstand, pulling open the top drawer.

*Holy shit.*

A large blade in a sheath greets me. And a pistol. I shut it and check the second nightstand. Another blade. I slam it shut and head for the desk, jerking on the drawers. They're locked. I knew that, though. Right?

I don't even bother with his computer; I don't have the password.

However, I *do* return to his nightstand, lacing my fingers around the pistol, tucked away in a holster. I pull it out, and check that there's one in the chamber. There is. This man lives loaded and ready to go—and I can't necessarily let myself become suspicious over that thought alone.

I lived that way. Before all my guns went missing.

Tucking the gun back in the holster, I hook it to the front of my shorts backwards, so that it's hidden by my baggy T-shirt. I swallow hard, knowing that this is probably a terrible idea, stealing a gun from Henry.

But it's not like I'm going to use it on him—I don't think so anyway.

My mind flashes to the moment I pulled the trigger in Mason's direction. I push it away, the anxiety threatening to return. I unlock the door, and swing it open, startled to see Jude standing there, his eyes narrowed at me.

"What're you doing?"

"Um, I was getting dressed?"

"I heard drawers opening."

"I was putting Henry's shirt back," I lie, and I'm pretty sure Jude knows it's a lie, but he lets me pass by him anyway. "I was thinking about taking Duke for a walk," I chime, spotting my dog still curled up on the couch.

"I can't let you do that."

"Why not?" I demand, a burst of courage coming from nowhere as I spin around to face him. Unlike Henry, he's not intimidating to me. He's tall and lanky, and well, comes across like a puppy.

He raises his brow. "Henry doesn't want you to leave."

"So *you* take orders from Henry?"

He purses his lips. "No. He's my partner, and depending on the moment, sometimes he takes orders from me."

"Does he listen?"

Jude's cheeks redden. "Sometimes."

I can't help but kind of smile at the embarrassment. It's almost endearing. "I don't think he'd listen to me, either."

"Ha," Jude snorts, shaking his head. "I think the man would burn down an entire village for you in a heartbeat. All you'd have to do is ask."

"That's intense."

"That's what Henry is."

We stand there, staring at each other for a few moments longer. A million questions swim in my head as the beats of silence pass. But as I open my mouth to ask, starting with my phone that suddenly isn't working...

Jude speaks first. "You want coffee? I have a strong feeling you'll be waiting up, too."

I nod, feeling the gun still lodged in my pants. Duke stays asleep on the couch as I slide onto one of the bar stools and Jude starts the coffeemaker.

"Henry is complicated," Jude begins, letting out a sharp exhale as he faces me. "But I can tell he's trying really hard with you."

"Has he ever done it before?" I don't really know what that means, *trying with me*, so I let the question land vague.

"Uh, no." Jude laughs. "I don't even know the last time Henry *spoke* about a woman, let alone brought her to his house."

"I'm here for the book, though."

His laughter fades. "Right. Okay."

I narrow my gaze. "He admitted that he wanted me when we met."

"And maybe that's why he stuck to his terms. He wanted *you*." Jude hesitates after he says it—like he might say something else—but then clamps his mouth shut, grabbing two coffee mugs.

"My phone isn't working," I tell him as he sets them on the counter.

He spins around instantly, his eyes flashing with something I can't read. "What do you mean it's not working?" "There's no service."

"Let me see it."

I dig it out of my pocket and slide it across the island to him. "I don't know what's wrong with it."

His brows furrow as he unlocks the screen, heading straight for the settings. "Have you tried turning it off and back on?"

"Yeah, and it didn't fix it."

"That's weird." He slides it back to me. "Maybe you got your SIM card wet?" The confusion on his face feels genuine, and I let out a sigh. Maybe they aren't somehow magically messing up my phone.

"I went on a walk with Duke, but I don't think I got it wet."

He nods, grabbing the creamer. "How do you like your coffee?"

"Just a little cream, not much."

"Got it." He pours the creamer, stirs it, and then hands it to me. "We can get you a new phone tomorrow. Don't sweat it."

"Why did he take a gun with him?" I blurt out the question and Jude once again lets out a sigh, like I'm a nagging toddler.

Jude takes a sip of his coffee, sets it down, and then leans toward me. "Why do *you* have a gun in your waistband?"

My cheeks grow hot. Maybe I'm not so smooth. "I..."

"I'm not going to take it from you," Jude laughs, leaning back. "I don't think you'd shoot me. Better you have it, anyway."

"Why?"

"That's a question for Henry. I think I've probably said enough for one night." He downs the rest of his coffee like it's a shot, and then heads over to the keypad beside the glass door.

I sip on the warm liquid as Jude punches in a code.

"*System armed,*" a robotic voice says. I don't know why it leaves me unnerved, but it does. Jude, however, seems as calm as ever, stretching his arms over his head.

"I'm gonna shower really quick. I'll come back down afterward and I'll be downstairs until Henry gets back. You might wanna get a bigger shirt, by the way." He gestures to the front. "It's too easy to see." With that, he disappears, his footsteps on the stairs the only evidence of where he went.

"This is weird," I mutter to myself, feeling uneasy as I slide off the stool. I grip my coffee and slip past Duke, who's out like a light. I consider waking him and making him come with me but decide he's really not that far away.

I enter my room, returning to the writing desk and staring down at the notepad, covered in notes. I haven't gotten nearly as far as what

I should have by now—and Henry hasn't made a single mention of it.

And maybe that *is* a red flag.

He's paying me a lot of money to be here and write a book, but other than the first night, he hasn't spoken of it. I don't know how I feel about that. But I also know now that he wanted me from the beginning...Like when we met?

My head aches as I try to put it together like a puzzle missing half the pieces. I reach for my laptop, and open it, deciding maybe I can at least check my work email. I click the browser, and it opens.

*Sorry, cannot establish a connection.*

I refresh the page, rolling my eyes. But the message pops again.

"Ugh," I grumble, clicking on the little Wi-Fi icon. It pops up. I double click it. "No internet connection," I read aloud. I lean over, checking the card I'd found on the desk with the Wi-Fi password. I disconnect and reconnect.

Nothing.

I reboot my computer. Nothing.

My head falls to my hands out of frustration. I let out a sigh, and then stand to my feet. *I'll just have to go find the router.* I pull the bedroom door in, step into the hallway...

And the house goes pitch black.

# Twenty-Five

## Henry

"So, here you are." Luca chuckles, his dark eyes studying my face. His jet-black hair is slicked back, and a shadow of facial hair lines his jaw. In comparison to him, I'm an angel, and evil radiates out of him like heat from a furnace. The man has no limits. He cocks a brow at me. "I was wondering when you'd show up."

I shut his office door behind me. "Just tell me what you know, Luca. I need to get back to the house."

"To your plaything?"

My stomach knots up. "What're you talking about?"

"The woman at your place."

"I don't—"

"She's in the file, Henry. No need to lie to me. I turned it down."

"Why? We could've fucking worked this out," I bark, slamming my fists against his desk. "I need to know who got the assignment."

"I. Don't. Know." His expression darkens, and while I consider us friendly, we handle things differently. "I respect you too much to kill you—and that's what most of this community feels. I have no idea if anyone will accept it."

I shake my head, running my hands over my face. "I slipped up somewhere. Someone knows my identity."

"You know how many hits I've had on myself," Luca says with shrug. "You know the drill. You find the one who placed the order, and you take them out before their people take you out."

"Why would he let them do it? He's blocked hits before."

"The Big Man?" Luca chuckles. "He's just a fucking psycho like the rest of us. He makes his money sitting behind a computer and dishing it out on the dark web. He's a master hacker and business owner. That's it. The only reason he's ever blocked a hit is because of pure amusement or hatred for whoever placed it. And for the record, he's never blocked a hit on me. I think the bastard gets off on trying to kill me."

I bite down on the inside of my cheek, not in the mood for humor. "I need to know who ordered a hit on me, Luca. How the hell do I do that?"

His impish smile fades to something more serious. "I've always had to get it out of the people showing up to take care of the job. Honestly, you're lucky this is the first time it's happened to you in the eleven years you've been doing this."

I nod, but the timing is horrible. "What were the files sent with the link?"

He taps on his computer and turns it around on the desk for me to look at. "I should've deleted this, but I encrypted a copy when I downloaded it. I knew you'd need it. It might get us both in trouble, but you know, you *are* my friend, Henry. As soon as I got it, I declined the invite and called Jude—but you know it bounces right to the next."

I lean over the computer, scrolling through the contents of the file. It's full of photos, but they're all from the last twenty- four hours. Most are of the house for layout purposes. And sure enough, there's a shot of Lydia leaving the house with Duke—and then talking on the phone as she heads down the beach. I swallow hard, wanting to murder whoever took those pictures of her. "This must have something to do with the most recent hit."

"Someone probably didn't like how you took care of it—or that you killed him in general."

"Who would even know?" I look up at him, and he shrugs.

"No matter what we like to think, there're eyes *everywhere*. We always want to believe *we* are the eyes, but we're just one set."

"Yeah, but now what?"

Luca meets me dead in the eye. "You pack her up and get her somewhere safe. You gotta ditch all technology. Check everything for bugs. You know the drill. You may have to separate."

"I can't...She has no idea what I do."

Luca chuckles. "So dump her off and let her suffer the potential consequences, or I guess tell her the truth. I would suggest the first option, personally. There's a reason I don't let pussy become more than just that. *Pussy.*"

I'd fucking burn myself at the stake before I dumped her off. "I'll figure her out."

"You must like her."

I ignore him, staring at the pictures. My stomach has that same nagging feeling, tugging at it. How could this happen? I make mostly flawless hits. Is this because of Carlson? Is it *Mason?* Was I *that* careless?

"Henry," Luca's voice cuts through my spiral. "You're my only friend in this fucked up underworld. You tell me to go, and I'll hunt this dipshit down."

My eyes flicker up. "I'm not going to ask that of you."

"Then let me figure out who it is, okay? Your head's shattered. Take the woman somewhere safe, send Jude here. You lay low. When we figure it out, you and I will take care of it. Two guns are better than one."

"I don't like that—"

"My mentor did it for me the first time I had a target on my back. I lost him, but he saved my life. I always said I'd repay it. Let me do this for you."

I narrow my eyes at him. "So, you *are* soft."

"Fuck off," he growls tossing a pen at me. "You're the closest thing I have to family other than Manny."

I chuckle, thinking of Manny, Luca's partner. We all operate much better with eyes on the outside. "Thanks, man."

"Outside of your head being a wreck," Luca begins, leaning back in his chair, "you look good. You get laid?" He shoots me a grin.

"Shut up," I snap. I pull out my phone, half-tempted to text Jude or Lydia. I expected to hear something from them already. I scroll over to the security app with my cameras.

"My new assignment is wild."

"Yeah?" I respond blankly as the app loads, the bar reaching three-quarters of the way, but not going any further. *What the hell?*

"Yeah, target is a cute little writer with a major inheritance."

I close out of the app and reload it, my frustration growing—but I didn't miss his words. "A writer?"

"Yeah, scheduled it out, too. I'm not supposed to make a move for a few months. It's a strange one."

"What's his name?"

"Oh, it's a *she*."

"I don't wanna hear about it," I grumble. "You know I don't take on women."

"Yeah, I know you're picky."

I don't hear his next words as I read the message on the screen. *Could not connect to cameras.* My stomach clenches. I scroll to Jude's phone number and hit the call button.

Straight to voicemail.

*No, no, no. Lydia.*

# Twenty-Six

## Lydia

I hear the footsteps before I make out the figure running toward me. I squint in the darkness, assuming it's Jude—but the closer they get, it finally clicks. And within seconds, my body is in motion. I barely make it in my room before slamming the door.

*There's no lock.*

I grip the knob and press my back against it, trying to settle my racing heart. A sardonic laugh erupts on the other side.

"You must be the toy," a voice sneers.

My eyes squeeze shut as I fumble with the gun in the front of my shorts. *Where's Jude? Where's Duke?* I can't imagine my dog sleeping through something like this. But then again, Mason broke into my house while I was sleeping, and I'm certain he never moved...

But he knew Mason.

My head spins as the knob twists. I do my best to hold it, my eyes blurring with tears. I can't hold the door *and* the gun.

"I'm gonna get in there, sweetheart, whether you want me to or not."

"I'm not alone here," I shout through the door.

He bursts into laughter. "I don't need long."

A force blows from the other side, and the door cracks. It jars me backward, the gun knocked from my hand and sliding across the floor. The light from my computer screen illuminates a man with a black mask hovering above me. He tilts his head at me as I scoot backward, trying to put eyes on the gun.

"You're a pretty thing, aren't you? No wonder Henry keeps you to himself." He hovers over me, and I now see just how large this guy is. He's every bit as big as Henry, and potentially twice as wide. And it looks like there's some sort of rope or rag in his hand? I can't make it out very clearly, but every ounce of common sense tells me it might be how I die.

The scent of cigarette smoke hits my lungs as he lunges at me. I throw my weight to the right, nearly missing his grasp, but his hand collides with my ankle. He drags me toward him, and I brace as he comes at me with whatever the material is in his hand. It's not rope. I have that much figured out now.

It's soaked in something as it brushes my nose. Just the scent makes my head light. I curl my fist and punch as hard as I can. My knuckles connect with the side of his mask, but it feels like I just struck metal. A cry escapes my lips, and he cackles down at me.

"Can't hit me, baby," he groans out as liquid drips from my knuckles and down my arm. My attacker comes down on me, his knees pinning my thighs as that fabric sinks toward my nose again. I turn my head and shut my eyes for a moment, just long enough to flick them back open and catch sight of the pistol. It's within reach. I lunge my hand toward it, but he grabs me with an iron grip, dropping the fabric to the floor.

I scream out in pain, something sharp cutting through the skin on my wrist.

"You've got a lot of fight in you," he grunts as my other hand comes in, ripping at the mask on his face. It feels like a cage, and I slip my hand under it, going for his eyes. He combats it by rearing his knee up and slamming back into my thigh.

Tears slip down my cheeks at the agonizing pain radiating from the hit. I can't even scream at this point. I'm fighting a losing battle as he grabs both of my hands and pins them over my head. I wriggle, but it's worthless.

"You can't overpower me," he spats, his words laced with hate. "And you might not get death today, but you'll be wishing for it by the time I'm done with you."

"Fuck you," I snap at him, courage and anger boiling to the surface. He bursts into another breathy cackle, but in the lulls, I *swear* I hear something coming.

I lift my head and gaze toward the door, something drawing me to it. And suddenly, there's a large golden blur careening toward us. My heart jumps out of my chest as I recognize Duke.

With a growl and snarl, he lunges at the man above me, startling him enough to free my hands. Duke is met with a heavy arm, and I watch in horror as he's thrown across the room to the bed.

*This fucker just hit my dog.*

I shove myself back, and my hand lands on the pistol. I pick it up just as the masked man lunges toward me.

"*Lydia!*" I hear Henry's voice but it's too late.

I pull the trigger.

A gunshot explodes in the silence, and a splatter of warm liquid covers my face. The body drops, landing on my stomach. I hear a rush of footsteps, but the ringing in my ears drowns it out.

I shut my eyes and take a breath through my nose, afraid to part my lips. The sensation of warm, moist air tickles my forehead and

I open my eyes, gazing up at the muzzle of Duke. And the sight is instantly comforting.

"What the hell happened?" Henry groans from the other side of me. With a shove, he pushes the body off me. I shift my gaze to those familiar icy irises, filled with panic and rage. I lift the pistol from the floor and hold it out to him.

"Here," I choke out in a near whisper. "This is yours."

He nods, taking it from my hands. Even in the darkness, I can make out his expression. Henry's jaw is tense, his eyes glistening—but I don't think it's tears, unless rage causes that sort of reaction from him. His hand brushes my sticky hair from my face, and then slowly moves around my face and neck, as if he's checking for injuries.

"If you think I'm bad, you should see the other guy." I try to laugh, but nothing comes out.

Henry doesn't even react to my poorly attempted coping mechanism. I catch my breath, wincing as he lifts me upward. My head spins for reasons I don't understand, and he mumbles something under his breath that I don't hear.

"What's on that?" I point to the rag on the floor. My body begins to tremble, but I do my best to ignore it.

Henry glances down at the material. "Probably just chloroform." His voice wavers as he picks it up and tosses it to the side. "Everyone thinks it's some magical way to knock someone out, but most of the time it does nothing—unless they get a lot. And then it can affect the nervous system, lungs, and even kill someone."

I start to shiver more violently as Henry pulls me into his arms. "I don't know what's happening," I say through chattering teeth. My gaze shifts toward the body, and just as my eyes take in the shadow, the lights kick on. I gasp.

The man in the light is even more gruesome once my eyes adjust. His mask is black with crimson X's over the eyes. There's a massive hole in his throat. Blood pools beneath him, as well as being splattered all over everything close to me—including Duke, who's watching the two of us intently.

And now I just feel...*cold.*

# Twenty-Seven

## Henry

I could *murder* Jude for letting this happen, but as I glance over to his unconscious body, knocked out from a blow to the back of the head, I grimace. I'll deal with him later. Lydia clings to my chest, and her hands wrap up the front of my shirt in a fist. She's getting me covered in blood.

And I don't even care.

I angle my body so that she can't see down the hallway, taking her straight to my room. My head is spinning. I don't know why she had my gun. I don't know why Jude didn't sound the alarm system we have on our phones when something goes wrong. I'm lucky I saw the cameras disconnected.

And I'm lucky my girl is a fighter—and a good shot.

I let Duke into the bedroom, and while he got tossed, he's just fine. Other than being worried about his person, of course.

"I am, too," I tell him as I use my knee to open the bathroom door wider.

Lydia is still trembling in my arms. My mind threatens to bring back the trauma that started my career in killing—the feeling of a small, fragile girl shocked to the point they're not mentally with me. Maybe Lydia isn't the only reason I helped Carlson's widow. Maybe it's because I'll never get rid of that night.

I sit down on the edge of the bathtub and start the water. For the longest time, I considered getting rid of it and adding more cabinets. I guess it's a good thing I didn't. Turns out I *did* need it. While the bath is filling, I carry her to the shower. All of the blood needs to be rinsed off before I stick her in the tub.

No one likes to bathe in someone else's blood.

Well, I can think of one exception. But now's hardly the time for that.

"I'm going to undress you," I murmur to her as I gently set her feet to the tile floor. She nods her head, and while leaning against me, she tugs at her T-shirt. I help her, lifting it over her head. My eyes drop to the holster tucked in the front of her denim shorts, and I want to ask.

But I don't.

It doesn't matter why she had my gun. I'm just glad she did.

Robotically, she helps me remove the rest of her clothes, which I slide across the floor to a pile. They'll have to be burned, probably, but that's a task for another day. Whoever that fucker was that attacked us, failed his hit—but died before I could get any information.

*If he had any.*

I swallow hard, trying not to be aroused by the blood covering her body. She's a boss, and I'm proud of her. But I also know how tender this moment is. Killing someone for the first time is traumatizing—much more so than just shooting at some asshole's feet. I help her into the shower, grabbing the wand and rinsing her off.

She winces as I cross the gashes on her arms, and the blood on her knuckles.

"You put up a hell of a fight," I murmur, as she flattens her palm against mine. "You did good, darling."

Her eyes flicker up to mine, searching, aching, as she lets me see her most vulnerable. "I shot at him."

"I know."

"No, I shot at him...Before I came here."

"Your ex?" I refuse to say the dipshit's name, no matter what.

"They're going to think I did it," her words come out heavy. "They're going to think I had something to do with his disappearance. Both of them."

I release her hand, pressing both of my palms against her cheeks. "You didn't do anything wrong, Lydia. You protected yourself, and it resulted in that asshole having to bite the bullet. What you did for him was a favor to him."

Her bottom lip quivers. "How?"

"Because I would've made every breath he took until his death more painful than the last. I'd have made him beg for me to end it." I exhale and then brush my lips across the bridge of her nose. "I'll never let this happen again."

*I'll never let this happen again.* I've said the words before. I've made the promise. And I upheld it. I still am. My sister is safe, and she always will be as long as I'm alive.

I focus on washing the blood from her hair, and when I finish, I help her out and to the bath. She leans against me, her breaths shallow but steady. She's sore, I'm sure, but the most damage is the kind I can't easily see—or fix.

"Get in with me." Her words are in a near whisper as she tilts her head back, her eyes locking with mine.

"I can't," I tell her, disappointment thrumming through my body. "I have to go make sure Jude is coming to."

Her eyes widen. "Is he okay?"

I nod. "Yeah, he took a pretty good blow to the back of the head." *And might get a second for not stopping this from happening.*

Lydia sighs, and I help her into the warm water. As she slides down, her body visibly relaxes. It's a small win for such a bad fucking night. I lean over, kiss the top of her head, and then slip off for the bathroom door.

"Henry," she calls after me, her voice stronger than before.

I gaze back at her. "Yeah?"

"What do you really do for work?"

I look her dead in the eyes, and then exhale sharply. "I kill people, Lydia."

She stares at me for a few beats—and then bobs her head slowly. "That...That makes sense." Lydia pulls her knees up to her chest and rests her chin on them, ripping her eyes away from me and staring at the white wall. Her emerald irises grow distant, and my stomach feels sick.

If she can't handle this small dose of truth, then the rest will leave her in ashes. I knew I might break her, but I didn't want to annihilate her.

"Would you..." Her voice comes out like a mouse squeak. I spin around, preparing to answer another hard question, but she continues. "...get me a towel?"

I swallow the lump in my throat, and head for the black cabinets, pulling out a fresh towel for her. "I can warm it for you."

She shakes her head, avoiding my gaze.

*Right. I have to give her space.*

But not so much she can run away from me. She's the only thing that's helped me feel something after years of nothing but numbness. I don't want to go back.

I set the towel on the edge of the tub and then leave her there, letting her soak in the warmth of the bathwater *and* the truth bomb I just dropped on her. I close the door behind me, anger and frustration building in my chest.

I want to *hurt* someone for this.

A groan breaks my thoughts, and I rip the bedroom door open to see Jude propping himself up, his hand going to the back of his head.

"What the hell?" Jude wipes the blood smeared across his fingers onto his shirt.

The sight of him royally pisses me off, and in seconds, I'm standing over him, dragging him to his feet.

"What're you doing?" he shouts at me as I pin him against the wall, crimson smearing across the white surface.

"You almost got her *killed*," I exasperate, pulling him toward me and then slamming him back against the wall.

"Shit…Henry, I tried to chase the guy, and he just—I'm so fucking sorry." Jude's head drops, and I hate that he's so sincere. He looks back up at me. "Is she okay?"

I release him, clenching my fists at my sides. "No, she's not okay. She's messed up about shooting some guy in the throat when he attacked her—and now she knows what I really do for a living, too."

Jude lets out a ragged sigh, running his palms over his face. "This is bad."

"I have to get her out of here. We might have taken care of one threat, but you know once the news gets around he's dead, it'll just go to the next on the list—if it hasn't already. I haven't checked for wires yet."

"You just focus on getting her and yourself out of here. I'll take care of the mess."

"And then you're going to Vinita." It's a nickname for Luca's place, one that very, very few know. It's a safe place. For now.

"No other info gathered?"

I shake my head. "I'll go start packing."

"I know where you're headed, right?"

"Yeah, you know."

*And she's gonna be pissed when we show up.*

# Twenty-Eight

## Lydia

*He kills people. He's a murderer.*

But so am I.

The towel feels like sandpaper on my skin as I wrap it around my body. It's not comforting, nor is it a distraction from the utter confusion I feel. I *want* to be angry at Henry for lying to me about his job—but what for? If I murdered people for a living, I probably wouldn't broadcast that either.

The tile is cold and slick against my wet feet as I slip toward the bathroom door, pulling it open and peering out. My eyes land on Henry, who's throwing clothes into a large duffel bag. My heart trips over itself—the first sign that it's still beating. But...is he...*running?* Is it because I know the truth?

*Ugh.*

Even though I want to be angry and should be scared, I still, in this moment, feel nothing. Other than the fact that I need him now, more than ever. I drink in the sight of him, the blood smeared across his white T-shirt, and the way his biceps appear as taught as his jaw. The stress radiating from his movements is palpable. And for some reason, I have an urge to make him feel better. Maybe it'll make *me* feel better, too.

"Hey," I croak as I step out into the bedroom. "Where are you going?"

He doesn't look up as he drops a hoodie into the bag. "Away." The cool air in the room leaves my body chilled, and shivering, I take a step closer to him.

"Away to where?"

Henry licks his lips but keeps methodically packing. "I can't say. They may have bugged the house. Who knows."

I nod, swallowing hard. It's a lot of information to process, but the closer I get to him, the more I need him to look at me. The scent of his cologne grows stronger as I keep putting one foot in front of the other, closing the space between us.

"What're you doing, Lydia?" His voice is tense, low, and has a gravel that I've never heard before.

"Why won't you look at me?" I demand, no longer scared of the intimidating, murderous man. I mean, he might do it for a living—but we sort of have that in common now, right? Or maybe it's just the shock lingering in my system. Things still feel numb...

And I want him to fix it.

But he's ignoring me instead. "Go get dressed and packed."

"Why are you suddenly shutting me out?" I exasperate. "What changed?"

He tips his head away from me. "Please go get dressed. You need to take time and process what happened tonight. *Go.*" The rejection stings, more potent than the heartbreak of my lost six-year relationship. And I don't know why, but I can't let it go.

"I don't want to."

He stops, curling his hands into fists. "Why are you pushing me?"

"I'm not pushing you," I cry out, emotion cracking my voice. "I just want you to look at me, Henry. You can't do this. You can't just ignore—"

He cuts me off, his body on mine in moments, his fingers laced around the back of my neck. His nose brushes mine, and my breath hitches, but he stays emotionless. "I am *not* ignoring you. I am *trying* to give you time to mentally work through what happened. Killing someone for the first time is not something you just get over with a hot bath."

I dare him with my gaze, burning with a desire I don't understand. "Fix me, Henry."

"I'll only break you more," he murmurs, brushing his lips across my skin. His kiss is soft, nearly sweet. But I need it harder, the numbness threatening to swallow me whole.

"*Break* me," I whisper. "I need to feel something."

He rests his forehead against mine, his eyes closing. "I don't wanna break you because you need to feel something. I want to break you because you *want* me to."

A lump forms in my throat. "*Please.* I want you to."

Henry groans, his free hand slipping through the front of the towel, brushing my still-damp skin. "Fucking torture."

"Then don't torture yourself by saying no," I plead, my fingers brushing his stubble. He pulls me toward him, kissing along my jaw. With every moment of contact, his mouth connects with my skin a little rougher.

"We need to get going," he growls, biting into the skin of my neck.

"Then make it fast," I moan, as he slides his fingers between my legs. He rubs my clit with his fingers, while his mouth sucks hard on my flesh. I cry out as pain erupts from the spot. It's different than the pain of being attacked. It sends flames of arousal through my body.

"You're so wet," he groans, sliding two fingers along the entrance of my pussy. "I won't be easy on you." I bite down on my lip as he sends his fingers deep inside of me, the pad of his thumb colliding with my clit. "I want to do terrible things to you."

My eyes squeeze shut as he spins me around, planting my ass against his cock. I grind against him, losing control of my senses to the primal desire breaking out in my chest.

"I can make you feel again," his voice comes out threatening. "But is that really what you want, Lydia?"

I barely manage to nod as I moan out, growing close to an orgasm. My hips rock against his hand as I hear the sound of metal sliding against metal.

And then I feel something pressed to my neck.

"This is how I prefer to do it," he whispers in my ear, and I struggle to catch my breath as I realize there's a knife pressed to my throat. A tiny jolt of fear slivers down my spine. "One cut." He presses the tip to the back of my jaw. "From here." He drags it across my skin, leaving goose bumps in its wake. "To here." I gasp for air and cry out as I crash around his hand, my orgasm pulsing around his fingers. "Good girl," he growls.

Before I even have the chance to come down from the high, he slips a hand from between my legs and undoes his jeans, all the while leaving the knife against my throat. He shoves the tip of his cock through my wet slit, plunging inside of me. "Fuck," Henry slams into me, one hand squeezing my breast and the other holding the knife to my throat.

I take him over and over, and while he gets rougher, the knife remains pressed into my skin, unmoving. My cries and whimpers fill the room as I grasp the dresser, the force of his cock making my knees weak. His hand drops from my breast, wrapping around my waist to hold me up.

"*Henry!*" I cry out as he drives into me unabashedly, his groans primal and angry. His grip on me tightens, and consequently, the blade breaks my skin. I let out a scream at the burning sensation and Henry roars, ramming into me one last time. He drops the blade to the ground as he falls forward against me, releasing.

"*Lydia...*" he groans. He pulls out of me as soon as he finishes, spinning me around to face him. His eyes grow wide as my hand shoots up to my throat. I pull it away, relieved that it's only a small cut. "I'm so sorry, Lydia."

I wipe more of my blood on the tip of my fingers and shake my head as I press it to his lips. "It was exactly what I needed."

His lips part, sucking them into his mouth. My breath catches as his tongue runs along my skin. Henry's eyes stay locked with mine while he cleans my fingers off. Finally, I pull them away, and use my thumb to wipe away the red smear beneath his bottom lip.

"Thank you," I whisper, a small amount of relief pulsing in my veins.

"Don't thank me for ruining you," he tells me in a husky voice, brushing his fingers across the small cut. "Go pack. We need to go."

\*\*\*

Thirty minutes later, I'm climbing into an SUV I don't recognize with a driver that might be even more terrifying than Henry.

"This is Luca." Henry clears his throat from beside me, nodding to the dark-headed and black-eyed man in the front seat. He looks like he belongs in the mafia, his biceps nearly as large as my face. I want so badly to pull out my phone and take a picture to send to Emma...

But I don't think he'd appreciate that.

"You're looking stressed this evening, Lydia." He cocks a brow at me. "You should relax a little."

*What a compliment.*

I glance over to Henry, who's stifling a chuckle behind Duke sitting between us. I nearly smile at the rare sight, but then my mind reminds me of the assailant that fell on top of me—and whose body I had to step over while I was packing. Bile shoots up the back of my throat.

Swallowing it, I turn to Henry. "Where are we going?"

"To your ride," Luca answers before Henry can. "Don't ask any more questions. It's better to just go along and keep your mouth shut. It'll keep you out of trouble."

Henry gives me a look, and I fall silent for the next forty-five minutes, staring out the window as the car travels down the highway, the ocean view fading away. Luca eventually turns into a small airport, maneuvering through dark hangers until we reach a small private jet, parked out front of a large white metal building.

I want to demand from Henry that he tell me where the hell we're going, but I keep it in, resigning to leading Duke to the plane while Luca and Henry grab bags. They talk in low voices that I can't make out, and so I focus on getting Duke settled. I pull my phone out one last time, checking for service. There isn't any.

I slide it back into my pocket and settle in, finding a seat on the plane. Fatigue pulls at my eyelids, but I'm too scared of what I might see in my dreams. Henry pats Duke, who's sitting on one of the couches, and takes a seat next to me.

"So…" I begin as his eyes rake over my body, pausing a little longer over the mark on my throat. "Where are we going?"

He cracks a small smile. "To see my sister."

I nod, resting my head on his shoulder. I close my eyes, and then let myself succumb to the fatigue I was afraid of only moments ago.

# Twenty-Nine

## Henry

"Are you from Oregon?" Lydia raises her brow at me as I bump the jeep along the gravel road, leading up to my sister's place. Her property consists of a ten acre, mostly wooded farm. The rural airport we flew into is only fifteen minutes away—and I did that on purpose.

I shake my head. "We're not from Oregon."

She purses her lips. "Okay...So then where *are* you from?"

"Nowhere."

"That's not an answer," she quips, her expression displeased as she folds her arms across her chest. "I'm literally riding in the front seat with a man whose career is a hitman—and now he won't even tell me where he's from. Grand."

I chuckle at her attitude, relieved to see she's still got a little fire. "For the record, I only say *nowhere,* because we never stayed in one place very long."

"Military?"

"No," I scoff. "More like career criminal."

Lydia nods. "I won't press."

"You can press," I tell her, eyeing the scab on her neck where I cut her. It makes me feel guilty—and aroused. Talk about complicated. I don't want to hurt her. I might not be able to manifest love, but I can try not to fuck her up.

Which I'm clearly doing a terrible job of.

"Okay, so where did you live? What was your childhood like?"

"Can't you ask me anything else?" I grumble as I pull up to the large, wrought iron gate and roll down the window.

"You said I could press. I'm pressing."

Rolling my eyes, I punch the code in and watch as the gate lurches. Cher doesn't get out much, and I don't blame her for it. I take a deep breath as I drive through the opening, and then stop to wait for the gate to close.

"My dad dealt drugs. Left my family when I was four or five—Cher was a baby. My mom remarried..." My body tenses as I think about it, and I white knuckle the steering wheel. "He, uh, wasn't a great guy."

"I see." Lydia grows quiet.

"They both passed away when I was sixteen."

Her brows crease. "I'm so sorry."

"Don't apologize." I shift my attention from navigating the rough driveway. I look over to her, but her gaze is focused outside of the car, taking in the Douglas Firs and Pines.

And the view is breathtaking.

Her eyes are wide, lips slightly parted as she drinks in the view in a part of the world I don't think she's ever been. My heart stumbles and flips over itself, and I place my hand on my chest. Maybe she's giving me a heart attack.

The two-story log cabin appears as we reach the top of the steep climb, and I hit the garage door opener attached to the visor of my jeep. I keep it at the airport and use it when I fly into town.

"This is beautiful." Lydia draws a deep breath. "I live in a log cabin, too." She smiles brightly, her eyes still sparkling as they meet mine. "It's not nearly this big, though." Her cheeks blush a deep crimson hue, and I can't stop myself.

I kiss her.

A light moan slips from her mouth as I bite down on her bottom lip, but I don't do it hard enough to draw blood—not now. She threads her fingers through my hair, sending a rush of arousal through my veins. If I'd been a crazed sex-hungry teenager, I'm pretty sure this is how it would've gone.

I break the kiss, and then push open the driver's side door. "Come on. She knows we're here already."

"Cameras?"

"Loads of them," I answer, gesturing for her to join me. There's only one hiccup with this whole plan, and as I swing the garage door open, it unveils itself.

"What the heck are you doing here?" Cher raises a dark brow, her pale skin looking as ghostly as ever.

"Good to see you, too, sis."

But she ignores me. Cher peers around me, her eyes widening as she catches sight of Lydia helping the dog out of the car. "What...What is this?"

"That's Lydia Waters," I answer her. "And Duke."

"Why are you bringing strangers to my house, Henry?"

I purse my lips, tempted to correct her but relent. "She's my...Um...She's..."

*Fuck.* What *is* she? *My soul.*

"Holy. Shit." Cher nearly squeals. "You have a girlfriend? And she looks *normal?* What madness is this?" She shoves me to the side, rushing to Lydia.

But then Lydia turns around.

"Whoa." Cher looks back at me, her excitement shifting to worry—and then rage. "That's *Piper Lewis.*"

Lydia's smile slowly starts dissipating as she clings to Duke's leash. "I...I am, yes..."

"I love your books," she says flatly.

*Shit.*

"But I have to say, you're a long way from Oklahoma."

Lydia tugs at the bottom of her sweater. "I am. You must be in the private group to know where I'm from."

Cher nods, narrowing her eyes as she steals a quick glance at me before looking back at Lydia. "I am. I recommend your book to just about everyone. Including Henry."

"I saw the note," she says, taking me by surprise. Lydia stands with her hip cocked, her eyes bouncing to me every few seconds. She can feel the tension. And I'm about to get ripped a new one before this is over—but hopefully not in front of Lydia. That would be too much for her to handle.

"Ah, so...How did the two of you meet?" Cher continues to block us from entering the house.

"We can get better acquainted inside," I cut in gruffly.

"No, I want to know how the two of you met." Cher glares back at me. "How did you meet her, Henry? Why is she here? A capti—"

"I hired her to write a book for me," I stop her.

Her brows shoot sky high. "*You* hired her to write a book? Since when does a hitman become an author? Huh?" She turns to Lydia. "You do know what he does for a living, right? He's not some—"

"She knows," I growl, placing my hands on Cher's shoulders and guiding her back to the door. "And she's had a pretty fucked up twenty-four hours so let's just lay off." I push her faster than Lydia and Duke can follow, lowering my voice. "Do *not* keep pressing the issue in front of her."

Cher jerks free of me, spinning around with rage in her blue eyes. "You did something to her, didn't you? What'd you do, Henry?"

"Stop whisper-yelling at me," I snap, just as Lydia and Duke step into the cabin.

"Your house is lovely," Lydia remarks, giving Cher a soft smile. I can tell she's trying. She's trying to ease the tension in the room. That's what she does.

"Thank you," Cher says, this time her tone more friendly. "I'm sorry for interrogating you. I just wanted to make sure you were here on your own accord."

"Kind of," Lydia's reply comes out awkward, and the guilt in my chest beckons me to speak. I open my mouth to say something, but Cher's glare silences me. She's not going to breach the subject. Yet.

Instead, she comes across even creepier than me entering Lydia's house without permission. "I have the same picture as you do in your living room." She grabs Lydia's hand and tugs her toward the sitting room. "In one of your pictures you posted in the private group, there was this old, abandoned house..." I can't hear the rest of what she says as they step into the living room, but I'm relieved to have a moment alone.

I spin on my heel and head back for the jeep to get the bags. I'm sure Cher won't go asking Lydia the story of us right now, so it's safe for me to leave the two of them together. I check my phone, but there's no update from Jude or Luca. I collect the armful of bags, entering back into the house with a grunt. I use my heel to close the door, surprised to hear laughter wafting through the house.

And it's a gut punch.

*This is what our life could've been like.*

I make my way through the kitchen to the living room, which now that I'm there, I realize is similar to Lydia's place— but only in the sense of the décor—and I guess the picture.

"I'm going to take these upstairs," I say to the two—well, three—of them.

Lydia gazes over her shoulder at me, a smile on her face. "I'll help you." Her footsteps are soft against the carpet as she takes one of her bags from my arms. "I need to know where I'm sleeping, anyway."

"I'll make coffee," Cher calls after us as we climb the stairs. "Or maybe you guys should just go to bed...It might be six o'clock in the morning but you two look like you need a solid night's sleep."

I nod to her. "Yeah, we'll see."

"Come see me when you're settled, Henry."

*And the hiccup shows itself again.*

She wants answers, and I'm not sure she can take the truth—and not try to kill me for what I've done. Out of the two of us, she came out okay.

Because I sure as hell didn't.

# Thirty

## Lydia

"Your sister is nice," I say as Henry drops our bags onto the floor. "I like her."

"She likes you."

"How do you know?"

"She would've said if she didn't," he chuckles, straightening up and rolling his shoulders. "But she's right, we both need to get some sleep."

I eye the bed uneasily as he flips back the covers and strips out of his T-shirt and jeans. I pour over his frame, taking in his tattoos and taught muscles. "Do your tattoos have any meaning?" I ask, my eyes lingering over the dragon on his chest, taking in the way it seems to be staring right at me.

He looks up at me and cracks a smile—but it doesn't reach his eyes. "No. They just cover the other shit I don't want to see."

"Scars?"

"They aren't scars if they can't be seen." He climbs into the bed, ignoring my gaze. He knows he's lying to himself. I know it, too, but I don't go there. We all have our scars. Mistakes. Things that make us ugly on the inside.

I shed my sweater, dropping it to the floor. He watches me as I peel my sports bra over my head, my breasts dropping free. I let out a sigh, ignoring the marks covering my body as I slip out of my jeans.

"You're beautiful, but I hate those bruises came from someone other than me."

I gaze up at him as I grab his clean T-shirt and shrug it over my head. "I bruise easy," I say quietly, gazing down at my legs. There're two asymmetrical purplish green bruises in the center of my thighs, and I shudder.

"Don't look at them, darling." A hand grasps mine, tugging me toward the covers. I let myself fall into bed, and Henry pulls me into his chest, kissing the top of my head.

"Why is someone trying to kill you?" I ask the obvious question—the elephant in the room that hasn't been spoken of.

"I don't know, but I'll figure it out. We'll be safe here until Luca and Jude pinpoint who's ordered it." He holds me tighter, his arm around my waist. "I don't know how long it'll be."

"My phone isn't working," I say blankly. I don't know why I mention it. But maybe it's a desperate grasp for normalcy.

He caresses my shoulder, chuckling. "I'm sure there's a spare around here. I'll take care of it."

And I believe him. I believe him to the point I let myself fall into a deep sleep, resting against his chest.

\*\*\*

*Oh, shit.* I grind my hips into the warm sensation between my legs, desperate to feel more. My eyes flutter open, moonlight streaming through the window of the room. I glance down, letting out a cry as Henry sucks my clit into his mouth while he slips a couple of fingers inside of me, waking me fully.

"You taste so fucking good," he growls, pulling away to run his tongue over me. He covers every inch of my pussy, as he wraps his arms around the tops of my thighs. He holds me to him, lifting my ass off the bed a few inches.

I arch my head back, letting out a cry as he sucks harder and then buries his face in me, drawing out my orgasm. I dig my fingernails into the bed as I crash around him. "*Henry,*" I moan out, my voice groggy with sleep as I ride the high.

His mouth cleans me up and his kisses land on my hips, stomach, working his way and taking the T-shirt material with him. I tremble beneath him as he slips it over my head. As soon as the T-shirt is on the floor, his lips are on mine.

Arousal floods back to my core as I taste myself on his tongue. His kiss is hot and heady, his hands raking over my body. He palms my breasts and then squeezes my nipples, his cock brushing my entrance.

"I couldn't wait any longer," he murmurs, burying his face in the nape of my neck as his cock presses into my pussy. "I needed to fuck you, darling. It keeps the nightmares away."

I whimper in response as the weight of him crashes into me, but it's fleeting as he grabs my hips and rolls us. I'm caught off guard by the motion, now straddling Henry's hips. His eyes gleam up at me, and his fingers pour over my skin.

"Fuck me like the good girl you are," he demands, grabbing my hips, lifting me up, and then slamming me down on his cock. I cry at the depth, my fingernails breaking the skin of his chest. I roll my hips, and his eyes become heavy, focused on my face.

As I rock and grind against him, his fingers brush my face, tracing my lips and then shoving a finger inside of my mouth. I suck on it, and he groans out with satisfaction before pulling it from my cavity. Arousal begins to build again in my core as I move against his body, stimulating mine as I fuck his.

I grab his hand resting on my breast and bring it up, placing his fingers around my throat. His lips part as he understands what I'm asking for, and he squeezes, cutting off my oxygen. Heat floods to my pussy, and my eyes close.

"Keep them open," he demands. "You look at me when we do this." I force them open, black stars dotting my vision, desperate for air. He lets me have it as soon as we lock gazes. "That's a good girl." He rams his hips upward, and it takes me by surprise, jarring my body so hard that I feel light in the head. "Come on, darling, give it to me."

Anger flurries in my chest, as if I'm not doing it good enough. My eyes flicker to the nightstand. And I see it, the metal blade glistening in the light of the moon. I swallow hard, lean forward, and latch onto the handle.

"What're you doing?" he demands, his cock dropping from my pussy. "We're not—*fuck!*" I slam back down on him, meeting his neck with the edge of the blade, while his fingers are wrapped around mine. "You devil of a woman," he groans, as I roll my hips with renewed confidence. His grip loosens on my throat.

"It's only fair I get my turn," I pant, pressing the blade into his skin. I don't know how much pressure it would take to break the skin, but the sight of it against his neck turns me on. We're in a standoff, strangulation versus the knife—and the fire in his eyes tells me he loves it.

He tightens his fingers, cutting off my air supply, and I respond with the blade, indenting his skin. He swallows hard, his breath hitching as his legs tense beneath me. I feel myself growing closer to a second orgasm, and he cuts off my air supply, my head growing light and vision hazy. I do my best to hold the knife.

"Come for me," he instructs, his voice husky. "Come all over my cock, darling." He sounds distant, but just as my vision goes entirely, he lets me breathe—and my body trembles, an orgasm washing over me. I still my hips as I pulse around him, my scream drowning out his growls as he follows my lead, filling me with his release.

I collapse forward, and he catches me, planting a kiss on my mouth. I suck in a long, deep breath, refilling my lungs with oxygen. My heart is still racing, my body sweating, and as I pull away to sit up again, I freeze at the sight of blood.

"It's okay, darling," Henry chuckles darkly as I pull the blade away from his neck. The silver metal is laced with crimson, and my eyes widen. "It's superficial, and I loved it."

I study his face for a moment, still straddling him. And then I do something insane. My tongue runs along my bottom lip as I bring the knife to my mouth, keeping my eyes on Henry's. He audibly swallows as I run the cool metal across my lips, covering them with the warm sticky liquid.

"Oh *fuck*," he tremors beneath me as I clean up the copper-tasting blood with my tongue. I find myself aroused by not just the action, but the hunger and lust flooding Henry's expression.

I then lean over and kiss Henry, letting him taste his own blood on my tongue. I set the knife on the nightstand while our lips are still locked, and he sits up in the bed, his arms wrapped around me and his cock still inside.

"You're perfect, Lydia," he groans, breaking our kiss and resting his head in the nape of my neck. I wrap my arms around him, lingering in the moment as we hold each other. And I forget how messed up my life is.

We stay that way for a while, until finally breaking apart. I slip into the bathroom to clean up and I hear Henry rustling around in the bedroom. Once finished, I peek out at him, surprised that he's fully dressed. My heart drops.

"Where are you going?"

"I have to talk to Cher," he says, his voice flat as he runs his fingers through his hair. His neck is free of blood, but the T-shirt laying on the bed isn't. "I'll be back in a little while. You need to focus on getting more rest."

I shake my head. "I don't think I can...I don't think I can sleep without you."

His face softens as he comes to me, pulling my body into him. "I'm just going to be downstairs. You're safe here. I promise." He kisses the top of my head, breathing me in. "You're everything to me, Lydia."

I tip my head back. "Already?"

He chuckles. "I don't play games. I decided you were it the moment I saw you. I can deal with whatever you carry, whatever quirks you have, as long as you're mine. I'll clean up and cover anything you do—anyone you kill. I'm not sure I can exist without you, anymore." He doesn't give me any time to respond, kissing me once more and then slipping out of the room.

My eyes linger on the door even after he's gone, my head spinning at his words. They're heavy and intense—just like Henry Bayne. But after everything that's happened, they feel *right*. Maybe I can't exist without him, either.

# Thirty-One

## Henry

How nice of you to finally show up to chat," Cher laughs as I enter the library on the second floor. I knew that's where I'd find her, immersed in one of the hundreds of books that line the shelves. She puts a title I don't recognize on the table and folds her arms across her chest, leaning back in the black velvet reading chair.

"I had to get settled."

"Oh, don't patronize me, Henry. I heard you fucking her. The whole state of Oregon probably did."

I crack a smile and shrug. "We have chemistry."

"Do you? Or did you rob her of her sanity?"

"It's not like that," I sneer. "We're just—"

"You're just what?" She stands, her expression filled with anger. "Living in some delusion? You hired her to write a book for you? But did you really? I never would've given you it if I'd known you were going to do this!"

"What the fuck are you talking about?"

"I looked it up, Henry. All I had to do was search for missing people in her area, and *bam!* There's her fiancé. You killed him, didn't you? And then what? Used your connections to clean it up?"

My jaw tenses. "He was bad to her."

"Oh, right," she laughs manically, running her hands over her face. "Bad to her how? By existing?"

"He tried to hurt her," I say blankly. I mean, I knew Cher wouldn't swallow it easily, but I wasn't expecting a blow up. "After they broke up."

She narrows her eyes at me. "And when did they break up?"

"After we met."

She groans, shaking her head and placing her palm against it. "I don't even know what to say to you. Did you really want a book? Or did you just want her?"

"You know the answer to that."

"No, Henry, I don't think I do. Because for my *entire* life, I knew something was fucked in your head, but I didn't realize you'd go to this length to get what you want—and the worst part is, it's my fault."

"It's not your fault," I argue with her. "She makes me feel like less of a monster, Cher. She makes me fucking *feel*. I didn't force her to be with me."

Her lips purse and eyes close. "I hope you didn't. Our mother would be rolling in her grave if you did."

That stings.

"She'd be rolling in her grave, anyway."

Cher meets my eyes. "Yeah, but I think she knows we're doing the best we can with the cards we were dealt."

"I don't know. Maybe had I not become—"

"You became what you had to," Cher stops me, sighing. "And I'm sorry for saying you're fucked in the head. We both are."

"You're not wrong. But also, for the duration of this, let's *not* talk about her ex-fiancé."

Cher gives me a warning look. "I can't promise you that. If I find out she's not here because she *wants* to be, I'll have her on the next flight out. You don't get to be God, Henry. That's not how love works."

"I don't care how love works. I'm not *in* love," I snap at her, my eyes flickering to the massive windows. "That ability died in me long ago."

She presses her lips together in disapproval as I turn to leave, muttering something under her breath. I don't stay to figure it out. The brief conversation has the wheels in my mind turning. I know it's only a matter of time before Lydia puts the puzzle pieces together.

Which is why her phone is no longer working.

I had Jude take care of that for me—as well as limiting her internet usage, including controlling her email. And it's a good thing with all the press about Mason. His family has gone off the rails, but thankfully, I've kept her safe from it all. I need to give her time to accept this life with me fully.

And then I can tell her the truth.

My stomach knots up as I open the bedroom door, my eyes landing on Lydia, lying there in the bed. Her eyes are closed, her breaths steady, and I linger there for a few beats, watching her. I still *want* to love her, but my wants are just that. *Wants.* Just because I desire something, doesn't mean it comes to pass.

And I'm reminded of that as I strip down and climb into bed with Lydia. I pull her body into mine and wrap her up, burying my face in her hair and breathing her in. I have to handle telling her the truth so fucking delicately when the time is right—when I have the mess of the hit taken care of.

Because I really don't know how to exist without her.

And I don't even want to think about going down that road.

# Thirty-Two

## Lydia

It's been three weeks.

And I've been so lost in Henry, that I haven't even bothered with the outside world—though I did send Emma and my mother an email, letting them know I was taking some time to write. Though I haven't. Maybe it's the healing I needed after taking the life of someone—that I've now concluded deserved it. Or maybe I am just lost in falling for someone who seems to see me more clearly than the rest of the world does.

Well, and Cher has a killer library.

"Do you know when my phone is supposed to be here?" I ask Henry as he pulls a book from the shelf, flipping it over.

He shakes his head, squinting as he scans through the blurb on the back. I've decided that while he might be a murderer, he's also kind of freaking adorable. And to be honest, I think I might be in love. He's attentive, careful, and somehow he comes across more sincere than anyone else I've ever met.

"It'll be here in a couple days, probably," he mutters, putting the book back in its place.

"I should probably get to work on your book," I say blankly, not having even cracked open my computer as I process the realization of my feelings.

He glances over at me, laughing. "You can do whatever you want, darling. You can never start it for all I care. Write whatever you want. I'll still pay you. You can have whatever I own."

I shake my head. "You're ridiculous with that talk."

"Nah, we'll be married the moment we get out of here."

My heart stutters in my chest. "Yeah, right." I turn my attention to the back of a book, swallowing hard. My cheeks flush as he comes to me, wrapping his arms around my waist and kissing my neck.

"We will."

"What about a proposal?"

"I'll give you one if you want one."

I frown, tipping my head back to catch his lips. "I don't need one. I don't even know if I want one," I sigh, cringing as I think back to the last one. "I'd rather just make it to the freaking altar."

"Mmm," he hums into my skin. "Have I ever told you how much I'd like to bend you over in this room and take that tight pussy of yours?"

Goosebumps trail along my skin, but the sensation is cut short when his phone rings. We exchange a glance, and he gives me a light kiss before pulling it out of his pocket. I see the *unknown caller* on the screen, and watch as he answers, putting it to his ear.

"What do you have for me?" he asks his voice breathy. He's nervous, and I feel for him. He hasn't shown it, but I know his head is swimming over this. And as much as I want to hang around and listen, I decide to give him space, slipping out of the room and closing the door. I head for our room, deciding now is as good of time as ever to start on the book.

However, as I step into the room, Henry's laptop catches my eye. It's sitting on the bed, and I glance over my shoulder. I don't know why I feel a pull toward it, but I do.

And I give in to that tug, walking over and opening it up.

I press the enter key, my stomach churning as the password comes up. I try his birthday, first—which I know thanks to Jude. It doesn't work. I almost give in, but then for shits and giggles, I try *my* birthday. I laugh as I hit enter, expecting it to kick me out.

But it unlocks.

*That's a weird coincidence.*

My heart jumps to my throat as the screen opens to the desktop, and I'm left gaping. I nearly close it, a part of me wanting to ask Henry *when* he changed the password to my birthday. I mean, he knows it. I've told him.

But...something still doesn't feel right.

Hand sweating, I brush my finger along the pad, moving the cursor over the files, and my head feels light as my eyes land on the one that jumps out at me.

*Lydia Waters.*

I double click it.

And then I almost lose my breakfast. What. The. Fuck.

I start scrolling through the contents, pouring over every ounce of information. The man has *everything* about me in the file. There're pictures of my house, my *birth certificate*, medical records—how the hell did he get those? Every picture I've ever put on social media, and a lot that were just on my phone.

*Maybe he did this after we met.*

I click on the files origin, fear pulsing through my veins as I read the date.

*December 11, 2023.*

Nope. Nope. Nope. This *cannot* be real. That would make this file from before he ever even messaged me about writing a book. That would mean that he saw me before he *really* saw me. I snap the computer shut, unable to stomach looking through the contents anymore. My brain tries to come up with scenarios, justifying the action.

I mean, he could've just been curious about me after reading my books—and he's a hitman, so he's an in-depth researcher. I nod to myself, but I lunge for the closet. Along with a duffle bag—which contents I watched him empty—I *know* he also carried in a backpack. I rip the door open and kick on the light, my eyes scanning the walk-in area.

*Where is it?*

I finally spot it on the top shelf. There's no way I can reach it without help. I grab a wire hanger, undo it, and hook the strap, pulling it down and catching it.

*Maybe I shouldn't do this.*

*So what if he has a file on me?*

*He probably has a file on everyone he knows.*

But my shaking fingers still pull the zipper free of the front, largest pocket. And what I find leaves bile rising in my throat. My fingers connect with a mask and pull it out.

The same mask I saw weeks ago.

I drop it to the floor as a sob breaks loose in my chest. It was never Mason stalking me. It was Henry.

*Did he come into my house? Take my guns? Did he...*

I rush the bathroom, vomiting up the avocado toast I had for breakfast. Hands shaking as I wipe my mouth and flush the toilet, I step back into the bedroom, but this time, I'm *not* alone.

"Are you sick?" Henry asks, concern filling his face.

My body trembles under his gaze. I'm *mortified* I was too stupid to put it all together. I should've known. I should've put the pieces together—but I was too blinded by *him*.

"Lydia," he says softly, taking a step toward me.

I take one back, ramming my back into the edge of the bathroom door. "Don't," I warn him. "Just fucking *don't*."

His eyes widen, and he glances at the open closet door, the mask lying on the floor. "It's not—"

"Don't tell me it's not what I think it is," I sneer through the tears rolling down my cheeks. "*You* were the one who stalked me. Put the rose on Duke's collar. Stole the guns from my house. Scared me with *that*." I point toward the closet. "It was *you*, not Mason."

He lets out a sharp exhale. "I did what I had to."

I blink a couple times. "You did what you had to? Are you fucking serious? You *terrified* me!"

"You rejected me. I had to change your mind."

"You lied," I whisper, choking back the cries that rattle my ribcage. "You lied to me about it all."

"I did what I had to, to have *you*. I *need* you. You wrote me before you ever even knew me, Lydia."

"Those are just stories!" I break into a sob.

"Let me hold you before I have to go," he says, his voice full of anguish.

But as his hand nears my body, I swat it away, anger flushing my face and smothering my cries. "You called me while he was talking to me outside my house," I say, memories flooding my head. "Why'd you call me? Was it because you could *see?*"

His silence is everything. It's fucking *everything.*

"You fucking psycho," I shout, trying to split the distance and slip through the opening. He lunges for me, grabbing me, and pinning me against the wall. He does it so gently that it makes me hate him even more in the moment.

"Don't go there, Lydia," he snarls, though his eyes are riddled with hurt. "Don't make me go there."

But I can't stop.

"You probably tampered with my phone, didn't you?" I throw at him, fresh tears rolling down my cheeks as the realization hits me like a freight train. "How'd you kill him, Henry? Did you force him to go to Vermont? Did you call one of your killer friends? Lure him there?"

"He never went to Vermont," Henry's voice is low and emotionless. "It's artificially manipulated footage."

*I can meet you in three hours.* The text slams into my brain like a piano falling from a second story window.

"You killed him the morning he left my house."

Henry's jaw ticks. "I did what I had to do."

My brows shoot up. "What you *had* to do? You *had* to kill my ex-fiancé? Stop making it out like you had to do it!"

"I'll brutalize anyone who's touched your body before me." His words are like ice, but the emotion in his eyes is anything but, his irises growing stormy. This time, however, I don't find it nearly as mesmerizing.

"Well, lucky for you, you've completed that task," I scoff, shaking my head in disgust. "He's the only person I've ever been with. Congrats. Now let me *go*."

His lip trembles, and I don't know if it's anger or hurt—or both. He releases me and grabs the backpack from the closet, shoving the mask back into it. I should be running, but instead I watch him, unsure of what he might do.

He looks up at me as he slings the backpack over his shoulder. "I can't let you leave, darling." Suddenly, the pet name feels condescending, making me feel *small*.

"So what? You're gonna just keep me prisoner?" I exasperate as he heads for the bedroom door, grabbing up his laptop.

"Until you get over this, maybe."

"What're you doing?" I demand, my chest filling with panic as he slips from the room, almost shutting the door in my face. I catch the edge, nearly smashing my fingers. "*What are you doing?*"

"What I have to." He shoves my fingers back and slams the door. And then I hear the lock click. From the outside.

# Thirty-Three

## Henry

"You can't expect me to leave her locked in there," Cher exasperates, chasing me to the garage. "It's cruel!"

"She'll run," I say, my undertone malicious and emotionless. Lydia sees me for what I am now, and if I let her go, I'll be forced to track her down. Forced to take her back. Forced to screw up the dynamic we have.

"Let her," Cher screams at me as I rip open the driver's side door of the jeep. "Let her run from you! Let her choose."

"Fuck off," I bark at her. "She's never had a choice. It's always been mine to make. She's not going anywhere. I might have made her *think* it was her choice, but she was always going to be mine. No matter what." I hate the tears I see in my little sister's eyes. I hate the way they make me second guess myself. I hate that they're because of *me*. I want some people to hurt, but Lydia and Cher? Never.

But Lydia called it what it is.

I'm a psycho. Might as well live up to the title.

"Don't do this," she pleads, grabbing the door. "Don't be like him."

"I'm *not* like him," I shout at her. "I don't—I don't do what he did."

"Maybe not, but this…You're *better* than this."

"I'm better than nothing," I scoff. "I'm just a different kind of evil than the man who raised us. Still destined to destroy." She shakes her head, but I don't give her the moment to speak. "Don't let her leave or you'll have hell to pay, Cher."

The fire in her eyes tells me she'd pay it.

But that's just a risk I have to take, because I apparently have to learn lessons the hard way. Like for instance...

The woman I let go is the same one trying to kill me.

***

"You look like hell," Jude tells me as I climb into the passenger seat of the Tahoe. "Like *really* look like hell."

I glance over at him in the backseat and shrug. I'm not in the mood for chatting.

"He's going to stay in here while we take care of this," Luca tells me from the driver's seat as he smashes the gas and whips the SUV around.

"Okay."

"The guy who broke into your house to look around cracked pretty quick," Luca explains as he tears down the highway. "I pinned him. He was either Craigslist material or a rookie. Whichever he was, he's no more now."

"Mm," I mutter, glancing down to the pistol in my hand. My mind replays the terror on Lydia's face. The way she looked at me for what I am—a monster. I don't know why it stings. It shouldn't. Nothing about her reaction was surprising.

Well, other than she didn't try to kill me.

I had considered she might try, but even that would've been better than the heartache in her eyes. The way she smacked my hand away when I just wanted to fucking hold her. If I could just start over...

"She's probably going to know we're coming," Luca speaks into the silence. "We need to prepare for security at the house. Body-guards. Other hitmen. Whatever."

"We haven't been able to enter the house," Jude adds, looking at me. "She's got it under lockdown."

I nod, not turned off by the idea of entering a death trap. It might be the perfect solution. Lydia can hate me in peace.

"What's wrong with you?" Luca smacks me in the arm. "You're never this quiet."

"Just mentally preparing."

He bobs his head, accepting my answer, and we spend the rest of the ride in silence. An hour later, he turns into the neighborhood, punching in the keypad at the gate with ease— that's how Luca does everything. He could slaughter a whole town and never blink.

"No security outside," Luca says through gritted teeth. "I think she knows we're coming."

"Maybe we should go back." Jude's voice is full of annoying nerves. He's *not* made for the field.

"I'm not going back," I grunt, throwing open the passenger door. I grab my pistol and don't even bother with the mask. Fuck this woman. Fuck all the women who made me soft.

"Wait!" Luca shouts at me, but I don't listen. I sprint for the door. And as I press down on the lever, it opens.

*She's waiting.*

I slam the door shut and lock it, preventing Luca from coming in right behind me. Maybe it's better if I face this alone. I head straight for the room I killed Carlson in and am not surprised by the warm glow of the light. Pistol in hand, I turn the knob. For all I know, she might be waiting for me on the other side with a machine gun.

But as I push the door in, standing to the side, I catch sight of the woman. She's sitting in the middle of the bedroom in an armchair, dressed to the nines in a black gown.

Not a weapon in sight.

"I've been waiting for you," she muses, her eyes no longer dull or hazy. No, her hazel irises are sparkling under the glow of the lamp.

"Yeah? So you can kill me?"

She laughs. "No, I just needed to get your attention." I cock a brow. "My attention?"

"Yeah, and your little toy out of the way," she gleans, her face taking a jealous turn. "You don't belong with someone like *her*."

*Oh fuck no. What is this? A spurned lover?*

"You saved my life," she continues, her dark hair cascading over her shoulders, "and while I might have a few years on you..."

*Like a decade or two.*

"I think we could make this work. After all, my husband was an *evil* man."

Something is off in her voice. I divert my gaze as she reaches to flip her hair over her shoulder and stands to her feet. She has no idea what the hell she's doing—or maybe she does.

*She's not Lydia.*

And even at our very worst, her being locked in a room, I *won't* take someone else. I hear the zipper of her dress, but I don't look up from the pistol in my hands.

*Fuck her.*

"Come on," she purrs, the material dropping around her feet.

*Nope.*

"This is a mistake," I snarl, rage boiling in my chest. "I'm not going to do this. Get fucking dressed."

"Come do it yourself," she teases. I suddenly wish I hadn't locked Luca out. I wish he was storming through the door behind me. "Let me fuck you the way you deserve, *Henry*. You need a woman who's broken for real. Not a slut who writes stories about women like me, wishing she *was* me."

*Never. I'd never wish she was anything other than herself.*

But is this what being broken does to a woman? I shake my head, warring with myself as my gun raises. I hear the squeak from her throat. Guilt swirls in my head.

"He had more balls than you, you know. He knew I was poisoning him. Slowly, overtime. You took my moment from me, and now you owe me. You'll be mine. Get on your knees and—"

*I only bow for Lydia.*

Two shots sound.

And she falls to the floor.

The door opens behind me, as if on cue, and Luca steps in, his eyes wide as our gazes meet. "What'd you do? Make her undress?"

I shake my head, full of disgust. "She called my woman a slut."

"Tends to be what sluts do," Luca chuckles, stepping over the bleeding body. He remains there for a few moments, before using a gloved hand to brush the skin of her neck. "Cyanide."

"What?"

"She's got cyanide on her skin—and a rash. She was going to kill you...and herself." Luca turns to me, a grin flashing across his face. "What a way to go out. Good thing you're not a horny bastard."

"No kidding," I grunt. I stay back from the body as he grabs a sheet off the bed and covers her. I pick up the shell casings from my gun, shoving them into my pocket. I had resorted to the fastest way to get rid of her, instead of opting for my blade.

And it's a good thing.

My mind flashes to Lydia's face as she cut me open with the same knife in my jeans. I don't think I'll ever be able to use it again. It's sacred now.

"I'll call for cleanup." Luca grabs my shoulders and turns me toward the exit. "I can tell you need to get back to Lydia."

I don't argue with him, but don't indulge in any details. I have no idea what I'm going back to. We leave the house in disarray and climb into the Tahoe.

"That was fast," Jude remarks with a chuckle.

"What's gonna happen to the kids?" I ask as Luca pulls away from the curb.

"They split as soon as Carlson died. They've been staying with a relative, disconnected from their mother. Some business associate actually called in the hit, by the way."

"Figures," I mutter as we pull away from the curb.

"Must've been a really dysfunctional home life," Jude continues, unnecessarily expanding on his thoughts. "I never understand how love can be so toxic."

"I do," I answer without thinking twice about it. That woman was the second person I've killed for Lydia—and the first woman I've ever taken from the Earth. And I don't regret it. The woman could've been in love with me and all my dark truths, but she would've met the same fate. Was it an overreaction? Maybe. Too late now.

"I take it things aren't so great at home," Luca chuckles. "I don't think it ever works out, honestly. You stepped up your game tonight, though. Turned down pussy and took care of the threat without regard for tits. It's impressive."

I purse my lips. "Just take me to the airport." I fall into silence, staring out at the blackness of the night. There's no stars in the sky. No moon. Just darkness.

And I let it pull me in.

I let it take me back to the night I saw my stepfather beating and raping my mother for the hundredth time. She fought like hell. She always did. But that night was different. She was *dying*. I took the knife from the kitchen of our upstate estate, snuck up behind him, and shoved it through his neck as she took her last gasp of air. I tried to revive her, crying as I threw my body into compressing her chest.

I had tried to call 9-1-1 right after—the way they teach you to, growing up. But he had disabled the phone line that night, and she was gone before I could do anything.

So, I set the house on fire.

I carried my sister out of that monstrosity with the twenty thousand I found in the safe. I got a fake I.D., changed my name to Henry Bayne, became two years older than I really was, and flew us across the country. My little sister became Cher because she loved the singer. And I wasn't going to argue with her over it. No matter how silly I thought it was.

I gave her a new life and a good education while I scrounged, eventually realizing the only skill I had to give was my ability to snuff the life out of people. I stumbled into the right people...

And here I am.

With a woman trapped in my bedroom.

\*\*\*

By the time I make it back to the house, it's the middle of the afternoon. The skies are overcast, but the little bit of sun peeking through paints a picture perfect view of the cabin. Cher is waiting for me in the yard with Duke as I pull into the driveway. I park outside of the garage, eyeing her as I climb out.

"I take it the hit on your back is null and void," she says, her voice soft, a tinge of relief in it.

I nod, my mind just as shattered as it was before. "Is she still up there?"

Cher nods, her eyes filling with tears. "I told her the truth, though. I told her the truth about you. She deserved it."

I look away from her. "That's fair."

"She needs to know *you.*"

"I think she gets it," I grumble, warring with the emotions destroying my heart. "I'm a—"

"No, you *think* that's what you are, Henry," Cher cuts me off, her voice wavering as a tear slips down her cheek. "You saved my life. You knew he was coming for me after he wore her out—he said so."

I shake my head, trying to block out the painful memories of the conversation I'd overheard the night of my first murder.

*I'll take her now that you're worthless,* he had screamed at my mother.

"You are capable of love." Cher grabs my arm. "You *love* me. You put me in the best schools while you never finished your education. You bought me this place when I got laid off from my job. You set the world on fire to keep *me* safe. You didn't do it for you. You never put yourself into the equation—and *that's* what love is. It's not obsession. It's not forcing someone to stay. It's letting them go."

"Stop it," I choke out the words, meeting her gaze—one that so closely resembles our mother.

"I know you love her," Cher urges, holding onto me, begging for my attention. "I see it in the way you look at her. She makes you feel like a human being. That's why you're hanging onto her so tightly. Maybe at first it was a game—scaring her into taking the deal. But it's more than that now, isn't it?"

The temptation to break down beckons me, to let the gates open and all the darkness take over my soul, so I *don't* feel what I'm feeling now.

"Henry, please," she clings to my arm.

I shake my head, push her away, and head inside.

# Thirty-Four

## Lydia

I hear him coming before he ever unlocks the door, and as the knob turns, I brace, wiping the sweat of my palms onto my jeans. It's not even been twenty-four hours since he left, and it's been a whirlwind. Especially when Cher offered me the truth. Then locked me back in here.

Her loyalty lies with her brother—and I can't blame her for that.

The door swings open, and in steps Henry, his eyes glassed over. He looks exhausted, wearing the same clothes he left in.

"Get packed," he says throatily.

Honestly, I'm too terrified to fight with him. I do exactly as I'm told, packing my bags in a hurry. He stands at the opening of the room, not even bothering to pack his own things—and that only serves to scare me further.

*Maybe he's going to kill me.*

I turn to him. "Your sister—"

"No," he cuts me off in a sharp tone. "Just fucking pack." My hands tremble as I follow his instruction, shoving everything messily into the bags.

A few tense moments later, I meet him at the door with my hands full. "Where's Duke?"

"Come on." He grabs the bags from my arms and motions for me to go in front of him. "Go out the front door."

My heart pounds wildly in my chest as I put one foot in front of the other, making my way to the main entry way. I step out onto the porch, spotting Duke playing fetch with Cher. He wags his tail and comes running up to me.

I want to fall apart and hug him, but I don't.

"What are you doing?" Cher demands, chasing after Henry. "Where are you taking her?"

He ignores his sister, pulling the leash out of his pocket and snapping it onto Duke's collar. He leads him to the jeep and puts him in the backseat. "Get in the car," Henry tells me, his voice devoid of any emotion still.

"You don't—"

"Stop," he cuts Cher off, giving her a look I don't understand.

He opens the passenger door, and while terrified, I don't see any other option. I climb into the car and buckle my seat belt. Henry meets my gaze for a split second, but I can't read the way his eyes are clouded.

"Where are you taking me?" I whisper.

He slams the door, and I'm left to sit there, mulling over what his silence means. He said he would never hurt me out of anger, but does numbness count? I swallow hard as he climbs into the front seat and starts the engine. Henry backs out of the driveway, leaving Cher to watch us with wide eyes.

And the fact that *she* appears worried, worries me.

"Henry, please." My voice breaks as he pulls onto the highway.

He shakes his head, the same way he did when he shut me out—the night I found out about his true career.

"You don't have to do this," I reason, reaching for him.

His jaw tenses as my hand connects with his forearm. "I do."

"You don't," I cry, tears spilling down my cheeks. "Cher told me about what happened, and I under—"

"Shut up, Lydia." His words are shocking, and I retrieve my hand, settling back into the seat. He's *never* spoken to me like that.

And I hate it.

He doesn't even care anymore, and that's more horrifying than if he held a knife to my throat. I fall into silence beside him, listening to Duke pant in the backseat. I focus my attention on the landmarks we pass, and it begins to grow familiar.

And it hits me in the gut when he tears into the airport entrance.

You don't kill someone at an airport with their luggage and dog—but also, he didn't pack... Because he's not going.

What's he going to do? Pay them to crash the plane?

*Or let me go.*

A jet is already parked outside when he pulls up alongside it. Without a word, he climbs out, ripping open the backdoor and grabbing Dukes leash. He hands it to one of the two men outside of the jeep, while the other grabs my luggage.

Henry then walks around to my side of the car and pops the door open. "Let's go."

I swallow the lump in my throat. "Where am I going?"

He looks me dead in the eye, his eyes finally flashing with something that leaves me aching. "Home. You're going home." He reaches across me and unclicks the seatbelt when I don't. "Come on."

I climb out with shaky legs, staring at him, but he's not looking at me. I feel my phone begin to buzz in my pocket—over and over. But I don't reach for it as I walk toward the stairs of the plane.

When we reach them, I turn to face him. "Why?"

He meets my gaze, finally. "Why, what?"

"Why are you letting me go? I could tell the po—"

"I love you, Lydia," he cuts me off. "I love you with every fucking ounce of my being. Every monster and evil inside of me bows to you. And I thought..." He pauses, squeezing his eyes shut for a moment and then looking away from me. "I thought if I broke you, you'd love me. But as it turns out, I was the one who was meant to be broken. And I'm the one who's sorry."

My mouth falls open. I want to scream at him, beat my fists into his chest for breaking my heart with a gut-wrenching speech. But I'm still so livid that he lied to me. Manipulated me. Took a life because of me. I feel guilty for what he's done to others, and that's not fair. I want to shout that at him and make him feel the pain he's caused me. I want him to know he messed me up worse than anyone else ever could've.

But not a word slips out of my throat. I'm frozen as he leans in, planting a soft kiss on the top of my forehead. And even as the fury thrums through my body, I still want to wrap my arms around him. I want him to be the one who makes it all go away. My life might've been rocked by breaking up with Mason—but that might've never happened had I never met Henry.

And I'm so torn.

So, I watch him walk away, telling myself that it's for the best. I watch him climb into the jeep. I watch him leave, taillights disappearing into the night. And only when he's no longer there, and the flight attendant taps on my shoulder, do I board the flight.

My head is confused and I'm still so freaking angry, but there's one thing I'm certain Henry's wrong about.

He broke me, too. And I fell in love with him, anyway.

# Thirty-Five

## Lydia

Six months. Half a year. Six *fucking* months.

Half a *fucking* year.

That's how long it's been.

I sit on my couch and stare at the TV screen as it plays a segment on Mason's body being recovered. A known serial killer in Vermont is charged for the murder. Today, the trial starts. Twenty-three more bodies were found in his backyard.

But I know the truth.

It's just another articulated plan by an organization that I know exists somewhere in the darker realms of society. They manipulate murders. They use sickos like this guy on the TV when they have to. When it serves them.

And I know he did it for me.

He did it to keep the attention off me when I returned home. No sheriff deputies came knocking on my door. No police interviewed me or asked me questions. No, he led them *right* to the body. By the time I stepped off the flight, Mason's body was discovered with a trail of clues leading them right to that backyard.

Duke groans as he shifts on the other end of the couch, eyeing me.

"You still miss him?" I ask, laughing emptily. I blink the tears away and pull out my phone, searching for someone to talk to. No one knows what happened to me. Not even Emma. They think I was grieving Mason's death in solace, not falling in love with someone else. Well, Emma thinks I fucked the grief out of my system.

And I let her think that.

She's going through enough as it is, trying to divorce Jared—and she thinks I'm better now than ever. Maybe I am. But it sure as hell doesn't feel that way.

My phone ringing jars me from my daze, and I pick it up, answering it when I see the private investigator's name. "Hey, Shana."

"Hey..." her voice trails off.

"You haven't found him, have you?"

She sighs. "Henry Bayne doesn't exist anymore, but I can't find an obituary or signs of death either."

*Of course.*

By the time I had wi-fi calling again as my phone rebooted that night, all signs of Henry were *gone.* I was left with nothing. There were no more properties, all ownership to other people—*real* people. There were no signs of Cher Bayne, either. It was as if neither of them ever existed.

"I'll keep looking into him. I think you got scammed. You know that happens sometimes."

*The hundred-fifty-grand in my bank account is* not *a scam.*

"I don't know, maybe we should stop," I say flatly, my eyes casting to my laptop. There's a completed manuscript on there. Because whether he cared or not, I wrote the book. I wrote the book for him—*of* him. I just haven't published it yet.

Because I'm terrified my plan won't work.

Shana keeps talking. "There's bound to be some trace of him, I just can't find any other aliases. Most of the time conmen have other names."

"He had another name years ago," I tell her. "But I don't know what it was." And that's the truth. Not even Cher told me the names they were born with. I've dug into the history of New York crimes, too, researching house fires that resulted in deaths.

But newsflash, there's a lot of them. "Do you know when that was?"

"No."

"Ugh, he's good at disappearing."

"Yeah, he is," I say. "Thanks for the update."

We hang up and I toss the phone down beside me, laying my head on the arm of the couch and squeezing my eyes shut. I forgave Henry once I made it home, once I was right back to the grind of daily life. He did what he knew how to do, but everything fell together when he told me he loved me.

And he let me go.

I can't sleep. I don't date. I don't want to connect with people. I coped by writing the story of a hitman, living life on the edge until he meets a writer. He does the wrong thing to win her over, but gives her exactly what she needs. She starts to realize everything she missed out on by settling. They fall in love. He breaks her heart. She forgives him.

*She forgives him.*

And he comes back. He comes back and tells her that he'll never leave. He vows to protect her always, to love her, and to take care of her dog. She tells him she accepts his darkness and loves him not in spite of it, but because it's part of him. And she loves all of him.

But that's just a book.

And *this* is real life.

A tear slips down my cheek for the first time in months, and I let the heartbreak slip under the blockade I've built around myself. I bat it away with the sleeve of my sweater. It's time to rip the Band-Aid off.

So, I know he's really not coming back.

Closure. I need closure.

# Thirty-Six

## Henry

"I hate New York City," Jude groans.

"Would you just stop fucking complaining about everything?" I snap as we step into a dive bar situated at the bottom of a high rise apartment building.

"We're not here for fun."

"All right, *Brandon.*"

"I hate that name."

"Well, beggars can't be choosers when it comes to swiping social security numbers. There're only so many people to choose from that fit the bill."

"You can still call me Henry." I roll my eyes as we head toward the back of the seedy bar.

"That's not even your real name, Dexter Murphy."

I try not to gag at my old name. "Shut the fuck up."

He bursts into laughter, but it quickly fades as we reach the back door of the bar. "Are you sure you wanna do this?"

I look back at him. "Yeah." It's a lie. It's a lie what he thinks I'm doing, too. There's no intel at the top of this place.

Just an escape.

"Good luck," Jude's voice drops an octave.

"You're a good friend." I give him a smile. "The best, actually."

His face contorts. "Okay, weirdo. Go get that flash drive. The hit is due tomorrow."

But there's no hit.

I created the link. Sent it to Jude. He can't open the final part of the link without the embedded password—on the flash drive in the interior of my jacket pocket. And when he opens it, it's just a letter. One for him. One for Cher. One for Lydia.

And my will, leaving all my things to the two women I love.

I give him a nod and slide through the back door, closing it as I head for the maintenance elevator. I step inside and punch the twenty-fourth floor. I could've let a hit go wrong, making everyone think it wasn't intentional. I could've pulled the trigger on myself. Sliced the jugular vein. Hung from a noose. I could've set myself on fucking fire.

But this is what I chose.

Twenty-four floors.

Twenty-four days spent with Lydia.

That's all it took for me to fall in love with her, and to shatter myself of feeling anything once she was on that plane home. I step out onto the top floor, heading for the penthouse apartment. It's mine. I bought it under my new name.

Just to jump from the balcony.

I punch in the code, and step into the fully furnished apartment, locking the door behind me. It's not cozy. It's not welcoming. It's cold and numb. Like me. I shed my jacket and lay it on the black granite counter in the kitchen.

Maybe I'm a coward for doing this.

But after disappearing the way I did, my death will give Lydia the closure she needs if she can't sleep at night, scared I might come back to haunt her. I make my way through the set of French doors, stepping out onto the balcony.

I breathe in the cool night air.

And the moment feels right. She broke me. And nothing else brings me the high that she did. I let her go physically, but internally, I can't. It's impossible.

I meant it when I said I can't live without her.

I lean over the metal rail, staring down at the cement, dotted with solar lights. It's gonna hurt like hell. I let out a long exhale.

I'll find Lydia in the next life. I'll make it right. I'll ask her on a date, or maybe I'll be where she is, and ask her to dance. I'll wrap her in my arms. I won't have to hurt her. I'll love her. I'll always love her.

My phone vibrates in my pocket, and I almost don't look at the screen.

But it's from Cher.

It's a link. I sigh at the bad timing but click on it. My browser downloads an eBook file. I raise a brow. She knows better than to send me this shit.

But then I see the author.

*She would.*

I read the title, *Don't Let Go.* And as much as I want to read into it, I know how these fucking pieces of literature work. You write what you've experienced in a way that romanticizes the depravity of the real thing. But I continue on, reaching the dedication page.

*To the one who revealed to me love isn't always black and white.*

"Poetic," I grunt, casting my eyes back toward the railing.

My phone buzzes with a second text from Cher.

*Just read the last chapter.*

Does it end with me throwing myself off a balcony?

# Thirty-Seven

## Lydia

I've done nothing but pace the floors of my living room since I released the book over a week ago. Ten freaking days.

And that should be enough time.

Deep down, I know he's already seen it. I know for sure Cher has, right? She follows my work. But maybe she stopped. How long do I wait before I write it all off? I mean, the first night, I left my freaking door *unlocked*. I just knew he would come back.

But he didn't.

And here I am.

"Going crazy," I tell Duke as I run my fingers through my freshly dyed hair. I lightened the blonde, hoping it would make me feel better.

It didn't.

It only serves to emphasize the circles beneath my eyes. I tug at my sweater and blow out a sigh, glancing up at the clock. It's nearly midnight. It's time to call it for the evening. I may not sleep, but I have to try.

It's time to start moving forward, and while that's not happening right now, it will eventually, right? Time heals everything.

*And sleep serves to numb it.*

However, just as I head to my room, Duke runs for the back door, whining.

"I just let you out," I groan, my shoulders slumping as I make it to the back sliding glass door. He scratches at it with fervor, while I remove the extra lock in the track. I join him and pull back the curtain—and then gasp.

*Holy shit.*

Fear pulses through my body at the sight of a shadow on the other side. A sharp breath escapes from my mouth as I stumble backward, but then, as the realization settles in...

All the fear washes away and I nearly fall apart, hands shaking as I fumble with the lock and rip the door open.

"So, who goes first?" Henry eyes me as he steps into my living room, his face alight with amusement. "Shall we play it out like the book?"

I start to laugh softly, tears spilling down my cheeks as he clears his throat. He leans in to me, brushing his fingers across my cheeks to wipe them away. I open my mouth, but I can't get the words out. I can't even believe he's standing in my living room right now.

"Okay. I'll start then. Lydia," he breathes out, letting out a chuckle. "I love you. I vow to always protect you, cherish you, fuck you, and to never let you walk this Earth alone again. Oh, and take care of the dog. And by the way, my birth name is Dexter Murphy—horrible, I know. And also, I *can't* live without you. Was that close enough to the line in the book?"

I grab the collar of his shirt and pull his lips to mine.

He's *never* leaving again.

Even if I have to be the one who locks him in a bedroom.

# Epilogue

## Henry

"Do you think this looks okay?" Lydia steps out of our bedroom, wearing a black dress, clinging to the curvature of her hips and ending at her upper thighs. I take in the sight of her, including the sparkling diamond wedding band on her left hand. It only took me two weeks after showing back up at her place to put it there.

"You know..." My voice trails off. "I think it'd look better on the floor."

She makes a face like she might smack me. "It's my first girls' night out in almost two years."

"Yeah, I still don't know if I should let you go."

"You, Jude, and Luca were invited."

"Yeah, but seeing them with their women grosses me out."

"They probably say that about us, too." She walks toward me, climbing into my lap and planting a kiss on my cheek.

I breathe in the scent of her perfume, wrapping my arms around her waist and leaning into her. I kiss her neck, tasting her. "You sure you don't want to skip it, stay here, and let me steal your breath away? I'll even let you leave the dress on," I murmur into her ear.

She giggles, tipping my chin up to meet her gaze. "I think Emma would be disappointed. She's still settling here in Oregon. And honestly, you *always* steal my breath away."

"Yeah, but I mean in the literal sense." I smirk, bringing her lips to mine. She sighs, kissing me heavily. I slide my hand between her legs, brushing against her underwear, already damp for me.

"Okay, maybe just a quickie," she whispers as our lips part and our eyes meet. "But then I really need to go."

"I'll drive you if you let me have my way with you for the next twenty minutes."

She flashes me a devilish grin. "Deal."

***

Hi! Thanks for reading. **If you've made it this far, turn the page, and enjoy the first chapter of *Killing Emma*.** I promise, you won't regret it!

Their story is already out and available on Kindle Unlimited and paperback. Jude's story, *The Huntress and Her Hound* comes out July 12, 2024. It is up for preorder now!

You can also connect with me on Instagram or TikTok. My username for both is @anniewildauthor. There are multiple books in the works, so if you loved it, follow me for more! You can also sign up for my newsletter at anniewildauthor.com.

I appreciate your support!

# Killing Emma: A Dark Captive Romance

*Luca*

I've waited over well over six months for this. Why? I don't fuckin'
know. I don't make the rules, and I was taught a long time ago not
to question the man who calls in the order. So, when he put a hold
on my target, I waited. When he said it's go-time...I went.

And now here I am with gnarly, thorned bushes tearing my black
denim and scraping my skin. It's uncomfortable, but the view into
Emma Nightingale's bedroom window?

*Impeccable.*

The glow of the setting sun gleams right into the room, illuminat-
ing the white walls of the pristine space with an orangish-pink hue.
The cast of light is nearly the same color as her fiery hair, cascading
down her bare back as she faces away from me.

Emma Marie Nightingale's pictures don't do her justice.

No, not in the slightest. Her porcelain skin is a constellation of
freckles, covering her body like the night sky dotted with stars. My
eyes strain to get a clearer view of her as she drops her black dress
to the floor. Her curves are soft, beckoning me to run my calloused
fingers along them and press my olive skin against hers—what a
contrast that would be. I imagine my body against hers, wrapping
around her five-foot-six frame with ease, while I slide my fingers

beneath the front of her violet underwear. I grit my teeth, warring
with the unwanted lustful thoughts.

I don't intend to defile her. I'll steal the light from her eyes, but
only out of obligation. I wouldn't *choose* to kill a woman like Emma,
but then again, for all I know, she deserves what she has coming.
Even women can be demons, after all. And Emma is beautiful
enough to be a siren, that's for sure.

But I've killed pretty women before, and Emma will be no different. They fight. They cry. They beg and plead...until they don't.
I bring them to silence. I lead them to the next life. It's nothing
personal at all. It's just my job, and it's one I do well. Call me the
Grim Reaper's right-hand man—or the Devil's. I'm friends with
both.

"Are you going in anytime soon, or are you just gonna spend
the night in the woods?" Manny's gritty voice chirps in my earbud,
breaking the fixation of my thoughts.

I blow out a breath and keep my voice low. "I don't know. It's only
six-thirty. I still have some time." My gaze continues to follow Emma
as she bends over, giving me the kind of view that makes my jeans
feel constrictive. I adjust myself. I rarely have *this* problem when I'm
stalking my prey—no matter how beautiful the target is. However,
Emma, while not necessarily conventionally pretty to the world's
standards, is strangely intriguing to me.

Well, and that ass of hers...*Damn.*

"If you give it another hour, it'll be dark. I've already disabled the
cameras, but she doesn't know. She hasn't even checked them since
I started keeping tabs on her...*months* ago." Manny's voice sounds
bland and unenthused. We're equally unhinged, and he doesn't get
into it until the real chase begins. All the backstory, tracking, stalking

is uneventful at best. I haven't even bothered with it. I have other priorities that come first. Besides, I have a feeling this one is going to be too easy. Emma has made it that way.

In the two days I've been here, I've realized she lives in oblivion, and I can't decide if it's a blatant disregard for her own safety or if it's because she doesn't care. Regardless of the answer, I could creep around here in broad daylight, and she wouldn't break from her meaningless, empty stares. I intend to change that though. I might not violate her body in a way that would satisfy my darker side, but I still like to have my own fun. Her sanity will slip before she leaves this world—if it hasn't already.

"When we get back to LA, Ivan wants to meet up with us," Manny's voice cuts in again. He's getting bored, and I don't blame him, but the mention of his mentor has my stomach immediately sinking with grief.

I lean against the rough bark of an old oak. "I'd rather skip it."

"He hates it when you skip."

"He hates me regardless," I grumble as Emma disappears from the bedroom, now wearing a pair of light wash denim shorts and T-shirt. She's probably headed downstairs to the kitchen—and then to one of the many bottles of wine she hides out of sight. She's done it the last two nights in a row.

*Damnit, don't get drunk again, Emma. It'll make this much less exciting.*

I breathe in deep and start to shift my position, staying in the woods that surround her three-story manor. The walls of her castle are elegant white brick, accented with black and speckled red in some places. Its historic façade is fitting for this part of Georgia, though I know the house was built less than ten years ago. However, her wealth is anything but new. She's old money—and has no living relatives. The fortune is all hers.

"Wonder if Jared is going to call her again tonight," Manny muses in my ear, and I shrug at the mention of the name. I'm not worried about her accountant husband. He's not really in the picture, but if he calls again, that *could* mean she drinks extra.

I frown. "I'll have to put it off if she's unconscious."

"Depends on what kind of fun you wanna have."

I curl my lip as I skate through the deep, shaded brush. "I prefer my women to be of sound mind."

"Yeah, right," he laughs. "You make yourself out to be some fucking deviant playboy, but I don't know the last time you even had *that* kind of fun."

"You do enough for the both of us," I quip as I settle in with the view of the kitchen window, stationed about one-hundred-feet away. There's a large line of oak trees giving me cover, the woods circling her manicured lawn. Her estate isn't far from the Blue Ridge Mountain Range, and I have to admit, it's a picturesque location. She has good taste—in that way. Her neighbors have equally enchanting homes, though they're all separated by tall fences and woods.

Another advantage for me. No one will hear her scream.

I run my tongue along my chapped bottom lip as I watch Emma open a new bottle of red wine. I can't make out the label from where I stand and I don't know if this is how she unwinds, but a bottle a night is a little excessive.

*It'll slow her down when she runs.*

That thought causes my heart to take an extra beat, my palms sweating with anticipation. I can't wait for the words to leave my lips...

*"Run, Emma. Run."*

But right now, she has no idea what's coming. Emma's thick lips purse as she pours an overly full glass, and she then sets the bottle down on her butcher block kitchen island. She stares into the liquid, and I can't help but wonder what the hell she's thinking—if she is at all.

*Is she missing her accountant ex-husband? Is she just that fucking lonely? Possible mental health problems? Or is* this *her happy? Fuck, she doesn't* look *happy.*

I don't know the answers, and I don't know why I'm wondering anything at all. Maybe it's because for the first time in my career, I actually *can't* figure out what type of fight she's going to put up when I wrap my fingers around her pale throat. Part of me thinks she might just close her eyes and let go.

And I don't like that. That's not fun.

"So, lunch with Ivan Saturday?" Manny's back in my ear.

I swallow the knot in my throat. "I don't want to go to lunch. I've already told you. Ivan fucking hates me, remember?"

"No, he doesn't."

My jaw tenses. "I don't like the reminder of my fuck up." He falls silent at that, and as the words leave my lips, my mind pulls from Emma. It flashes with the images of my mentor—my own fucking father—lying lifeless on the floor, covered in blood. It's amazing how many lives I can take and never think twice, but the life taken of someone I care about stays forever burned in my memory. It's my only crutch.

*Because it was my fault.*

I shake my head and force it away, thinking of Emma, sweating and bloody in my grasp, cut from the same briars that got me. Fuck, I want the sun to set now. I don't need any more alone time with myself or Manny, and as I shift my gaze back to the window, I nearly jump. Emma is standing right there, peering out into the evening as if she's searching for someone...

Something jars in my chest at the sight of the longing in her usual blank face. She can't see me. I know that, but there's still something unsettling about the sight, her hand resting against the glass—like she's in a fucking prison and she's rotting away inside.

My stomach tightens as her lips stay flatlined. I don't think she ever smiles. For some reason, I can't even picture the woman with a grin on her face. Well, an *authentic* one. I've seen plenty of photos of her; a terse, fake smile pulling upward at her mouth in an almost painful way. I feel something. I push it away.

"I'm ready to move," I grunt, no longer enjoying the view in front of me. Emma can't be a person to me—she can't. She's just another body to add to the count, and it's time to carve that notch into my headstone. She's already affected my dick once today anyway; I don't need her to reach any deeper than that.

I push myself off the tree I was leaning against and roll my shoulders. My traps are tense and tight beneath my black sweatshirt. I dig the mask from my hoodie pocket and fasten it to my face. I'd like to go out with a bang tonight. I could use a good fucking chase—anything to get my adrenaline pumping. However, as I step out into the clearing, Emma spins away from the glass, missing me by only a couple of seconds.

*Well, that was fucking anticlimactic.*

"Someone's there," Manny's voice rings out with annoyance.

"Yeah, it's me," I scoff. "I'm going to kill the power."

"No," he snaps. "Get back to the tree line. It's the husband."

My shoulders fall. "Seriously? Why the hell is he showing up?"

"You act like I know or care. Just get back. I don't want the cops to be called. This is high profile."

"High profile?" I laugh quietly as I retreat to my cover. "This is *hardly* that. We've been here for two days, and the woman hasn't left her house. She hasn't even gone outside."

"Doesn't change the fact she's worth millions."

"With no one to give it to."

"Well, you're not wrong," Manny says. "In fact, I don't think anyone will miss this one. Her only contact is an outgoing phone call to an Oklahoma number every now and then—but not consistently. She's listed as a writer, but she doesn't have anything published. However, the last name *makes* her high profile, even if that's the only thing. The media loves rich white women."

"Sad," I mutter, but my voice is emotionless as I creep to the front of the place, careful not to lose my cover. More thorns tear at my jeans, but it's just another annoyance tonight has gifted me with. My eyes land on a white Porsche in the driveway. A dark-headed man, handsome by society's standards, stands outside of the front door.

"Come on, Emma. Just answer the door!" he snaps loud enough for me to hear. "I just wanna talk to you. I don't like the fact you're ignoring me. I hate this."

*Damn, maybe she is cold.*

Jared stands outside the house, his head falling to his hands, and I swear I hear his muffled sobs. I shift my weight uncomfortably.

I've seen men cry before—a lot, actually—but they're usually on the brink of death, begging for mercy. Mercy, I don't give them.

"Emma, *please.*" He beats his fist into the heavy black door, the sound of his desperation echoing into the still night. "I just wanna see you."

*Oh fuck, there are real tears.* I can see the moisture glistening as he looks back over at the door. Every ounce of my cold blood recoils.

"Can you see this?" I ask Manny, keeping my voice in a near whisper.

"Yeah, but I wish I couldn't. This guy is pathetic."

I nod, my curiosity piqued at the thought of this man showing so many emotions, and deadpanned Emma, always blank faced. "What's *she* doing? I can't see inside."

"She's standing two feet away from the guy on the other side, holding her wine and staring at the door. I don't know if she's going to answer it or not, but she looks stone cold."

"Unreadable Emma."

I can't wait to break her open and take a peek at what's inside.

\*\*\*

Get *Killing Emma* here.

Preorder Jude's story here.

# About the author

## Annie Wild

I love creating slow burn, dark, suspenseful, and broody romances that question just how far into the gray we're willing to go for love. When I'm not creating morally gray men and writing their redemptive arcs, you can find me going for hikes in the woods with my four dogs or immersing myself in a true crime podcast.

## Notes about my work and content:

**While I do love wading into the gray area of humanity you will not find the following in my works:**

- Nonconsensual intimacy (of any form) between the two main love interests.

- Incest of any kind between main characters.

- Situations involving minors/children. All main characters are mature, consenting adults.

**Darker themes between main characters that you might encounter in my books:**

- Stalking/obsession

- Hitmen, assassins, mercenaries, coldblooded killers (who do not practice sexual sadism)

- Some kinks (knife play, breath play, etc.) Kidnapping

- Motorcycle clubs and secret societies

**Note: Please read full list of content/trigger warnings listed in the description of any specific book before reading. Some contain nongraphic depictions of sexual assault and domestic violence (as well as other abuse).

Subscribe to my newsletter for more or follow me on TikTok/Instagram.